The Writer

PHILLIP BECKELHYMER

Copyright © 2021 Phillip Beckelhymer
All rights reserved
First Edition

Fulton Books, Inc.
Meadville, PA

Published by Fulton Books 2021

ISBN 978-1-63710-423-1 (paperback)
ISBN 978-1-63710-424-8 (digital)

Printed in the United States of America

Chapter 1

James came to standing just inside the master bedroom gripping a bloody double-headed axe as it dripped fresh blood into a puddle on the custom tile floor. He had no recollection of how he came to be there or where he came from. His mind was blank. Frozen in terror, slowly, he turned only his head to follow the trail of blood, which led out of the room and trailed back behind him before disappearing at the top of the stairwell. What or who was at the bottom of the staircase? He asked himself. Surely, whatever it was had to be dead, butchered more likely, by the looks of the thick trail of red liquid splatters neighboring the bloody footprints that led to his own feet.

Now standing in a puddle of the red paste, he looked up and saw his wife lying on the bed. For a split moment, he thought he had killed her but quickly rationalized there was no blood on her, the bed, or anywhere else in the room save the direction he had entered. She looked as though she was dead, however, lying there on her back, arms crossed over her chest like a cadaver in a coffin. His heart seemed to cease beating as he looked upon her before noticing the slow rise of her chest taking in air. She was alive. Thank God.

Oh, dear God, please don't let it be Chae that all this blood belonged to, not my little girl. That thought was immediately replaced with the realization that his daughter was out of the country, gone on vacation with her grandparents to the outback. He did remember that much. Normally he would not be happy that she was away, but right now he was overjoyed that she was safely away from here, over ten thousand miles away, on a completely separate continent. Another "thank you, God" was sent up.

As he began to move toward Shelia, he finally became aware of the approaching sirens. Lights danced off the walls and ceilings from the vehicles over the fields at the front of the property no doubt heading to his house. No one else lived out here. He and Shelia had purchased the 250-acre property because of the seclusion. They loved the privacy and intimacy the place provided.

He was not about living in the city, where houses were right on top of each other. Neighborhood dogs crapped where they pleased or neighbors mowed their lawns early weekend mornings, while others stayed up all night blasting music he hated. Block parties, community yard sales, and grill outs, which were actually an excuse for nosey neighbors to gain gossip and spread more. No, thank you very much.

He and Shelia loved the solitude they were afforded with the estate; however, that very solitude they so loved was being disrupted by a parade of police and emergency vehicles doing about mach 1. *What am I going to do?* he thought. *I can't go downstairs and out the front; the police will grab me for sure.* Plus, he did not particularly want to see what was possibly waiting at the foot of the stairwell, not knowing if he had killed someone or not. But the blood had to come from someone or something. Maybe more than one someone, he supposed. He had no clue of anything at all except that if he wanted answers, he could not let the police take him away. If he tried exiting the front, that would be inevitable, and he was not wanting to find whatever was at the foot of the stairs 100 percent. He needed to get somewhere he could think and start piecing things together. That would be impossible in police custody.

Heart racing, adrenaline pumping too fast for clear and rational thought, James went into a survival kind of mode. Adjacent the bed where they shared so many passionate evenings was a set of French doors that opened to a balcony overlooking the back of the property. The deck, which ran along approximately a third of the house, was seventy feet by thirty-five feet, and fifteen feet off the ground. Designed purposely without stairs so the house would be less accessible via the deck, James was wishing he'd chose differently now. However, standing six foot one, if he climbed over the railing, hung from the edge and dropped, the fall would be less than eight feet—just a short fall to a dry yard. From there, he could make a mad dash for the tree line.

THE WRITER

If he was able to make it that far without being seen, he could then try to get to the guesthouse which was on the other side of the property. The sirens were singing so close now there wasn't much time before they arrived. Walking to where Shelia lay, he tried to wake her but to no avail. She was comatose to the world, but at least she was alive. If he wanted to be with her again, he needed to flee right now and start looking for answers. James kissed her, told her he loved her, and promised he would fix this. As he turned and started for the French doors, a realization struck him for the first time. What if someone was still in the house and they got to her before the police arrived? Was he leaving her here in danger? No. For no reason he could ascertain, he just knew there was no one else here. Not sure how he knew, but he knew nonetheless. They were alone.

Confident as he was on the matter, still he ran to the master suite door and pulled it closed. As the latch caught, he punched in the security code. Inside the frame, he heard the mechanics turn and a short series of electronic notes, which were followed by a voice telling him the room was secure. Even if anyone had been in the house with them, they could never get into this room before the police got up here. In fact, the police themselves would need a battering ram to gain entry if Shelia isn't alert enough by the time they get up here to punch in the code herself, which seemed highly unlikely. So much for his custom-made door, which was the very least of his worries right now.

James gave her a final look, then hustled through the French doors to the railing. Lifting over the axe first, letting it drop alongside the house, he then stepped over himself, grabbed the edge, and lowered until he was fully extended. Pushing out away from the wall with his feet just hard enough to clear the hedges below, he let go and hit the grass. Without hesitation, he reached into the shrubbery and retrieved his axe.

Once again, blade back in his hand, James stepped away from the house and gave a final look up at the doorway to the suite. Adrenaline pumping so fast, heart accelerating even higher, the sirens almost deafening now, their approach imminent, James turned toward the woods, approximately three hundred yards away, and did the only thing he could do—RUN!

Chapter 2

James streaked across the moonlit yard, focused on nothing but the tree line, yielding the bloody axe as though it was a bloody baton and he was in some kind of morbid death race. Sprinting so fast, he felt as though he wasn't touching the ground, yet at the same time, the forest seemed to be drawing closer at a snail's pace. Lungs heaved, taking in the cool evening air in a manic rhythm. He must have looked like an insane madman, he supposed had anyone seen him, soaked in blood, racing through the moonlight carrying a bloody axe, which was still wet, and eyes the size of half dollars. Oh no, that didn't scream lunatic. He would have laughed at himself, finding it quite amusing if it wasn't so freaking horrifying. He grinned in spite of it.

Finally, after what seemed forever, he reached the destination he'd been sprinting for. What seemed to have taken forever was actually an amazing three-hundred-yard dash that would have shocked him to know the true time of. James reached the foliage hitting the mark he'd been aiming for, came to the nearest tree inside, and jumped behind it. He wanted to have a look back, plus needed to catch his breath before his lungs burst. *Wouldn't that just about suck*, he mused to himself.

No sooner did he turn to catch a glimpse, the first of many police cars come around the side driveway and into the yard flanking the house. Catching just a few seconds of breath and realizing no one was coming toward the woods, he knew he hadn't been noticed. He allowed himself only a few seconds more to catch enough wind so he could be off again. He had to get to the guesthouse. There he was, hopeful he could at least get out of these wet blood and sweat-soaked clothes and start some kind of process to figure out what was going on.

THE WRITER

James and Shelia lived in a small area outside of Cincinnati. Every local town officer as well as the local sheriff would most likely be at the main house. He doubted very much anyone would be waiting for him at the guesthouse. After all, it was really only accessible via the main house on the trail he was now running on to reach it. There was access from an old country road that was mostly gravel for almost half a mile that turned into a dirt road for another three-fourths of a mile, then came out on mile marker nineteen. There was no pavement between the guest house and marker nineteen, only a path of sort that James had cut himself and accessible only in a truck. Unless you were willing to get stuck trying to make it in a car, it was virtually unnoticeable as well. As mentioned, James and Shelia loved their privacy. Therefore, they kept that particular entrance a virtual no know.

Running at a steady pace over the trail was not difficult now that his eyes had adjusted to the darkness. The moonlight shone through the tree tops strong enough to reflect the dirt trail easily as it had been beaten down significantly over the many years since its creation. Actually, the run through the woods seemed to go faster than the three-hundred-yard psycho dash that took place beforehand over the empty field. *How's that work?* he wondered.

Arriving at the guesthouse, now approaching from the rear corner, he passed the garage where his truck was parked inside. First, before anything else, he had to get out of these awful clothes. Probably no time for a shower, but he couldn't stand the feeling of them on his skin any longer. He could run inside, peel them off, and jump in at least long enough to remove the worst of the red goo that was beginning to crust now. What in the world had he done? No answers came. The trip between the two houses hadn't triggered any sort of recollection.

James ran up to the door on the back of the house, which was closest coming out of the woods, and punched in the code. The lock turned, granting access, to which he obliged. Entering, then locking the door behind him, he leaned the axe against the door and began to undress, not fast enough to suit him. The blood, now cold, was also staining his skin. "So much blood," he said audibly. "Whose did it use to be?"

Now that he was back indoors and removing clothing, a stench was recognized, not noticed until now. The mixture of blood, sweat, and God-only-knew-what-else on him from the butchering was repugnant. He pulled faster at the clothes, leaving them where they landed, as he made his way to the shower. No time perhaps for his usual cleansing ritual, but at least he could remove as much as possible in his time allowed.

After a fast but thorough-enough scrubbing, James exited the bathroom for the bedroom and fresh, dry, bloodless clothing. After a fresh pair of shoes was retrieved from the closet, he headed to the kitchen for a glass of water. He was parched. As he drank the bottled water from the fridge, he thought to himself, *This is the greatest drink I've had in my entire life.* After guzzling three-fourths of the bottle, he came up for air, took a short gasp, then quickly finished off the rest before he grabbed a second. Taking more time now with the new bottle, he made his way to the office.

Upon entering the room, he discovered his laptop was open and a message waiting. Forgetting why he had come in here to begin with, now he was focused on his computer. It had been turned around as if to make the screen visible from the entryway. If it had been facing the way it was usually set, he'd have never paid any attention and would not have seen the message waiting for him. That might have been the best thing that could have happened to him this evening. *Who had been here?* he wondered. Without thinking any further ahead, he went over to the laptop. Not knowing what to expect, he opened the message. What appeared was something he never would have guessed or even believed.

First email:

> Hello, James. So glad you could finally make it. I imagine right about now you're wondering what kind of fresh hell you've gotten yourself into. Well, I may be of some service there if you allow. Do you like to play games, James? I do. I most certainly do, especially games that teach as you play. Don't you agree? Let's play a game, shall

THE WRITER

we. In this game I'm sure you will find answers to questions you are undoubtedly asking yourself as well as learning answers to questions you haven't asked yet or even thought of. I bet you want answers, don't you, James? Am I correct in assuming so? I have created a learn-as-you-go game just for you. Of course, you do not have to play. You could just leave right now in search of answers you seek on your own which could lead to weeks or even months of fruitless venturing where answers never materialize. Or if you choose to play the game, I would assist, and you will find the answers to all your questions before daybreak. That being said, there are a few rules to this game, as with any, that must be followed no matter what. So let me name them for you. Rule 1: If you choose to play the game, you must finish the game. You may not at any time for any reason stop participation of the game. Rule 2: You may not bring anyone else into the game. Rule 3: If you choose to play and learn, you will be timed from each location to the next where you will receive answers and further instructions on a laptop that will be awaiting your arrival. If at any time, you fail to make it to the given location in the time allotted, or should you decide to bring in outside help, I cannot promise the safety of your wife. Very easy rules to remember and follow but with very dire consequences. The choice is completely up to you. So what do you say, James? Do you want to play a game? If the answer is no, goodbye and good luck. If the answer is yes, scroll to the accept box and follow the directions that appear on the next screen. Oh, good luck in that decision as well. Hope to hear from you soon.

James stood there staring at the screen, dumbfounded. *Just what is happening?* he asked himself. He had no earthly clue. He awoke in the bedroom not recalling how he came to be there, covered in blood that wasn't his, holding an axe dripping with the red liquid, looking over his unconscious wife while police cruisers were boring down on his homestead. Fleeing from the second-floor balcony to the guesthouse on the opposite side of the property, in the dark no less, only to find an email from an individual whose identity he didn't know, asking if he would like to participate in a game whose directions sounded like those of a deranged lunatic's insane board game. *This is getting better all the time,* he thought. *This cannot be real.*

And what did he mean by saying he had a choice? Hah. What kind of a choice was it? Weeks, months, or longer looking for answers versus finding them in one night? That was no choice at all. And just what was meant by "cannot promise the safety of your wife"? Surely, she was in police custody already. This whole thing was completely nuts. Of course he would play. There was not even a doubt.

Who was the author of the email anyway? It hadn't given even a clue as to who it may be. Was it a man, woman, a group of conspirators, maybe a disgruntled employee or ex-employee? Too many questions circling in his mind and no kind of sense to be made of any of it. He needed answers, wanted answers, so yes, he would most definitely play the game. Unsure what was meant by finding answers to questions not asked yet didn't concern him. Getting answers now was all he thought to himself, and the sooner the better.

James moved the arrow with the mouse and clicked *accept* once more. A new message emerged, this time with an address.

> 212 Slane Ave., Cincinnati, Oh, 45153. You have 60 minutes to arrive. There you will learn some and receive further instructions. Do not pass go. Do not collect 200 dollars. Sorry, an attempt at humor. According to my calculations, it should be almost 12:15. The game started when you clicked on the accept box to play. So did the countdown, as will be the case through-

THE WRITER

out. The game will finish approximately 6 hours from now, depending on how long you spend at each location before hitting the accept icon on the laptop. You will have been taught things you sought answers for as well as those you did not. Best of luck, James.

James looked at his watch. It was 12:10—close enough. He grabbed his 9mm from the gun safe and two clips before retrieving his leather jacket from the closet. At the door where he had entered, he dug through his blood-soaked cargo shorts to fetch his wallet, keys, phone, and a knife he always carried just because he loved them, then kicked the clothing back so he could open the door. First picking up the axe, he turned the doorknob and entered the night. Pulling the door tight but not setting the alarm—the thought to do so didn't even register—he moved toward the garage.

In the garage, he headed to the work bench, grabbed a towel, then went to the basin washing what blood and tissue from the instrument he could in a hurry. Walking behind the truck, he threw the axe in the back of the bed as he went. Around to the driver's side now and entering the cab, James had a sense of déjà vu. That would not be the only time tonight he experienced it either, as he would find. Shaking it off, he climbed into the cab, hitting the garage opener as well as turning the ignition key. Both motors turned. One opened the door, the other running his Ram hemi. James plugged in the phone charger. With no idea what potentially lay in store for him this evening, he wanted to make sure he was able to reach the world of Google.

The 9mm was now in the console. Although he knew it would be the obvious spot to check if he pulled over, it didn't matter much, he figured. If he were to be pulled over tonight for anything, he assumed it was game over anyway. A quick prayer preceded his exit of the garage to the destination given him on the screen. It was an easy address to remember. It was the first of many properties he had accumulated since starting into the realtor business over twenty years ago.

At the age of twenty-two, he had begun with a single property that had turned into almost seventy-five properties now throughout the city of Cincinnati, everything from studio apartments all the way up to high-rise penthouses. The last several years now spent building and selling homes in the most prestigious areas of the city, as well as outside the limits like Indian Hill, where people had more money than they knew what to do with. Life had been good to him, and up to this point, nothing much had caught him off guard, but no one could be prepared for what was happening tonight. A feeling came over him that things would get a lot worse before the night was through too.

Again, as he drove, James wondered who might have left the email. How did they get past the alarm? Old business partners, old college buddies pulling a gag, perhaps a tenant felt unfairly evicted, an investor turned down—he could think of no one who was capable of this.

Racking his brain drawing closer to Slane Ave., he was unable to think of a single soul who it could be. Mulling over and over potential suspects in his mind, finally his thoughts turned from the stranger. Now James began to wonder what exactly lay in store at the address he was almost at already. *Time flies when you're losing your mind*, he thought. Whatever was waiting, he was sure it was not anything he wanted any part of even though it meant potential answers. His wondering what lay in store would soon be found out anyway.

The drive was a solid forty-five minutes, which didn't allow any extra time should something go wrong. A flat tire, a car wreck, or, God forbid, a sobriety checkpoint. What if any of those things happened? He dared not think such thoughts. He would cross that bridge if he came to it and prayed that he'd not have to do so.

Pondering as he drove, he could not recall any memory at all of how he got up to the room or even entered the house, for that matter. But trying to recall anything at this point was almost impossible. It was like trying to remember a dream that has passed while waking from slumber early in the morning. Just how much time had been lost from his memory, he couldn't say. Not positively. Amnesia, he guessed. Maybe that's it? No more time to dwell on that right now. He was approaching the first destination of the evening in which lay in store for his viewing pleasure the likes he never would have believed had anyone told him.

THE WRITER

The truck pulled slowly into the driveway, one faint light shown inside the house, and the outside light was on almost as though he was expected. James looked at his watch that was a Christmas present from Shelia and wondered if she was awake yet. *How much of this could she piece together?* he wondered. The time was 12:55. He'd made it with time to spare, which was great 'cause who knew how long it may take him to find the laptop inside or what he may have to do to retrieve it.

The pistol, taken from the console, was now in his hand under his jacket. James used caution approaching the front door and rang the doorbell. No answer came. This time he knocked loudly and waited. Finally, he realized he could not afford to waste precious minutes out here trying to enter any longer.

Zak Peterson was James's property manager. He took care of all the leasing, scheduling, maintenance, meeting tenants, background checks, evictions, court appearances for said evictions, hiring, firing, paperwork, all the bullcrap that James himself wanted no part of. James had no time for such things, nor did he want to fool with them for that matter and thus paid Zak quite handsomely to do the dirty work. Besides, James's time was spent in meetings. Endless meetings, it seemed—business partners, people who wanted to be business partners, bankers, investors, people that wanted to be his bankers and investors. He had meetings about meetings, he often joked. Therefore, he was not up-to-date on who presided at each and every property, but he did know who owned them, and all the leased and rental properties were on one master key. As he reached into his pocket for the key, he hoped no one had changed the dead bolt.

It did happen occasionally, but a lot less often now ever since he'd instituted a one-thousand-dollar penalty fee for any changed dead bolt without prior written consent, and subject for immediate eviction as well. Maintenance had been called on several occasions to a unit for emergency calls only to be denied access because the locks were changed which had led to significant water damage more than twice, and a fire that could have been avoided if they could have gained access upon first arriving. The water damage was more often than not a simple fix that would have cost a couple dollars if they could have gotten in, but had ended up costing thousands of dollars to the contrary.

The fire almost wiped out an entire building that had to have the tenants removed for several months and the interior of three apartment units completely renovated before they were livable again. Thankfully, no one was hurt, but tens of thousands of dollars were lost that time. Insurance covered a great majority on each claim, but as everyone knows, insurance companies are crooks and never pay more than they can get away with. Oddly enough, that still hadn't been what implemented the one-thousand-dollar fee with eviction looming. No, those reasons should have been more than enough, but what finally made him put the clause into effect, as in cases with many things, was bad publicity.

About ten years ago, at one of his properties, not far from where he stood now, an occupant had not been seen or heard from in almost a week. The tenant, known to everyone else in the eighteen-unit building as Boo, was a lonely old senior citizen who shared his one-bedroom apartment with a 115-pound pit bull named Tiny. After a few days of Boo being unnoticed, a smell began to permeate through the hallways. Maintenance had tried to gain entry a time or two, but the locks had been changed, and since nothing was leaking or burning, they didn't have much reason to drill out the dead bolt and destroy it for what the property manager assumed to be garbage coming from inside.

So the decision was made to wait, which was easy to do since it was Friday anyway. If no one had heard from Boo come Monday, Zak would make the choice to have it forced open or not. He was probably just visiting his daughter out of town as he did from time to time after all and forgot to take out the trash before he left. Boy was he *way* wrong on that.

Monday morning, the voice mailboxes on the office phones were full with messages from tenants from that building complaining about the stench. The maintenance guy for the majority of James's properties, Ned, arrived at eight o'clock that morning to Boo's apartment, but still no one answered. Given the go ahead to do so, he drilled out the dead bolt, having a new one already keyed to the master to replace it. The smell outside the apartment was so repugnant he could hardly stand it. Ned wanted absolutely no part of finding out what was creating the stench waiting to be found on the other side of the door. Plus he knew that Tiny was possibly in there just waiting for a patron to enter, another thing he wanted no part of. He hated dogs. Well, he hated other people's dogs. He didn't trust them, ever. How many times had he heard "that dog won't bite" only to almost be bitten? Who could remember?

After drilling out the dead bolt, the inside thumb latch fell to the floor as the outer cylinder and guard were removed. Now a stronger whiff of the stench could be enjoyed as it drifted through the new opening, almost making him vomit. Other tenants had begun to gather around by this time, and not wanting to be seen as a weenie for such, he was able to choke it back. Peering through the hole he'd just opened didn't allow for enough of a view to notice anything. Regretting and wishing he hadn't received the call on this one, he slowly started pushing the door open, cautious that Tiny could come running at any time to meet the visitor.

Ever so carefully, the gap between the door and the jam widened, releasing more of the putrid stench blasting Ned straight in the face on its way out. When it finally fully opened, Ned realized he no longer need fear Tiny. Boo's favorite companion was lying in the middle of the living room floor, dead as a doornail. Unknowing eyes now rolled back in his head revealing only the white, tongue crusted, stuck to the floor, and rigor mortis in full swing. Flies circled the decomposing carcass as something inside was crawling through the body, making the skin rise and lower, reminding Ned of what looks similar to a mole moving underground.

Venturing further inside, he noticed blood—a lot of blood—now that he was standing almost next to Tiny and had better view of the small abode. Bloody paw prints went back and forth throughout the place. From the kitchenette area, over to and on the couch, to the entry door, back across the living room, up on a chair, then across to the bedroom. Paw prints were on top of other paw prints throughout. The countertops and walls were smeared with it, and the bathroom door looked as though Tiny must have been trying to get inside. It was chewed, clawed, and looked as though it had been painted red from about four feet down. Inching near to the bedroom, almost certain now of what awaited, Ned peered inside. The sight that awaited him looked like something from a horror movie. *Carrie* came to mind rather quickly, the bloody prom scene being the first thought. The second thought was that what he was looking at looked like a giant piece of chewed bubble gum with a chewy liquid center.

Why didn't Ricky get the nod for this call today? Ned thought to himself. That's par for the course though. Ricky would have said Boo looked like a bag of smashed assholes though, instead of chewed bubble gum. Ricky was the maintenance guy of old who now mostly did nothing but the new house construction that James and some associates had started up. Something like this was what someone like Ricky deserved to find. He was the world's biggest a-hole. He hated life and everything in it, and was mad 24-7. He cursed like a sailor, talked to people like they were trash, and was so two-faced it was comical. If he was at the office, he bashed everyone that worked in the field. If he was out in the field, he bashed everyone in the office. Everyone knew nothing, and he knew it all. Anything went wrong, he threw you right under the bus even if you saw him do it.

Yeah, he was king jerk-off, class A all the way. No one could stand the guy or wanted to be around him. Unless he was around James—in that case, ass-kissing 101 was in session. Ricky was the headmaster, and everyone wanted to watch. Watching Ricky turn from king a-hole to the nicest guy in the world was hilarious. If they were together, it seemed like Ricky couldn't get his head far enough up James's ass to please himself. It was a pleasure for all who had seen it to behold.

James knew he was how he was, and he hated it and all the brownnosing too, but as big an ass as he was, the guy was a master carpenter who could build anything, worked endless hours, always on call, and if James said jump, Ricky did it. But since Ricky was somewhere else, head up James's rectum, Ned supposed he got the opportunity to choke back vomit and find this god-awful mess.

What remained of Boo, to Ned, appeared to be leftovers from multiple trips to the buffet bar made by Tiny. Boo's face and head

THE WRITER

were mostly left alone, except where a small portion of the jaw had been torn away while pulling at a chunk of meat around the shoulder. His stomach had been chewed through and all the organs eaten, as well as intestines. One arm dangled alongside the bed baring mostly bone from shoulder to wrist, with about three-fourths of the hand gone, leaving a thumb and more chewed bone. The man's legs were both picked clean down to the femur. Ned thought he'd never eat chicken legs again because that's what it looked like to him. Chicken legs that had all the meat removed but skin left on the bottom of the drumstick untouched. Boo's legs were virtually untouched below the knee as well.

Before he could note anything else visually of the corpse, he realized other tenants had entered the apartment. Ned snapped back from the ghoulish scene before him and began chasing them out quickly as possible with himself right behind them. As he still fought off the desire to puke, Ned grabbed the new dead bolt and threw it on while the tenants that had been in with him ran to tell the rest of the building what they had encountered.

Gina, who had been inside standing beside Ned before realizing he wasn't alone, was the building's busybody. That meant everyone that was home at this time would all know what had happened in about ten minutes. Anyone gone at this time would know about ten minutes after returning home. She had elected herself to be the head tattletale and was the main source of information between the tenants and the office. Something this juicy would keep her mouth busy for weeks to come, maybe months.

Ned called 911 and went through all the procedures of placing such a call, then waited for the EMT to arrive. The official cause of death, they would find out later, was a stroke. *Convenient,* Ned thought. The brain was the only organ not eaten, that was left to autopsy. All others had been turned to excrement, deposited on Boo's floor, or left undigested inside Tiny. If it had been a heart attack, he wondered how they would have figured that out. There were ways, he supposed, but there wasn't much left for testing.

While a stroke had taken Boo during the night, and he was laying there for days, Tiny had grown hungrier and hungrier. Long exhausting the food supply in his bowl, he was deduced to the only thing in the apartment he could attain for any sort of nutritional value. Not that there are a lot of nutrients in a dead senior citizen, but he had to eat something. Seven to eight days, the coroner had estimated the time of death for Boo. The dog had lived a few days longer, but having no access to water, the poor guy couldn't have lasted more than a few days, especially closed up in this basement unit next to the boiler. It was always hot in there. In a weird irony, all he needed to achieve water was for the bathroom door to have been open, but instead it had been pulled closed. Inside, all the water needed to survive would have been available. The toilet lid was up.

A story like that made headlines, naturally. James had received a ton of publicity because he owned the place, and a story like that takes a long time to go away. The incident had occurred almost ten years ago now. In that time, everyone who had lived there during the event had moved or been evicted, but the story of the man-eating dog that died of dehydration remained. Of course, after that many years of telling, retelling, embellishing the story by those who told it, the true facts of what happened had changed dramatically and resembled nothing close to the truth anymore. That is why James finally instated the dead bolt policy.

Now standing here at Slane Ave., James hoped he wasn't about to find the lock changed, or anything close to what Ned had found waiting for him on the other side. The key now inserted the cylinder, turned without hesitation, and he pushed the door open. For a split second, the thought of a chain or slide latch entered his thoughts, but it swung freely and without sound. James called into the house, but receiving no reply, pushed the door as far open as it would go and entered. With the pistol drawn and heart racing, he inched inside. The living room, immediately to the right, was as far as he needed to go before being greeted by the first of the evening's macabre pieces of finely detailed and twisted displays of human sculpture.

Setting in an office chair at his desk was a naked man. His eyes had been removed. Dried, crusted streams of blood, appearing mostly black now, ran from the empty sockets over sunken cheeks. The eyes themselves, James noticed, were positioned on top of the computer monitor and were looking back at the dead man, as to be watching him. One hand had been cut off and was now lying on the desk, fixed in a pointing gesture, back at the blind man as well. It was as if the creator of the ghastly piece was saying "I see you" to the deceased. *Or, eye see you*, James thought. The remaining hand grasped the mouse pad with the pointer finger on the click button. He approached hesitantly.

On the screen was a message addressed to James. Not wanting to touch the corpse, or anything else in the place for that matter, James used the pistol to guide the mouse over to the accept box, then pressed the click button with the barrel. The new screen opened with his new information, but he became distracted by the eyeballs atop the monitor once more. Attention diverted, drawn by the optic nerves that dangled down over the screen like pieces of crazy string and traced up to hazel eyes that no longer gave sight. The email opened and read.

Second email:

> Hello, James, nice to SEE you again. Lol, sorry, I couldn't resist the pun. Before you start feeling sorry for the man in the chair, allow me to tell you a little about him. The individual who resides in your residency is a major connoisseur of child pornography. He sat in the very chair he now occupies watching copious amounts of the filth for hours on end. That makes my stomach turn, James. Do you think anyone who does as such should be allowed to live? Obviously, as you can SEE, I do not. Fortunately for the man in the chair, he only watched the vile trash. Otherwise, his punishment would have been much more severe. I'm sure in due time, he would have moved on to doing more than just watching. Imagine, James, all the innocent children I potentially saved from being raped by this sexual deviant.
>
> As I mentioned before, you will learn things on your journey through this evening that you

may not want to know. The man in the chair dwells in one of your residences; rather, I should say *did*. Now I'm quite sure he resides in hell. I thought you may like to know who it was you were renting too. In fact, James, you rent to quite a number of unscrupulous tenants. The man in the chair will not be the only one you learn of this night. Now I'll give you an answer to a question I'm sure you've been asking yourself. Well, sort of. I bet you would like to know who I am. Would you like the answer to that, James? I will tell you eventually, but not yet.

What I will tell you is that you do not know me. You have never met nor seen me at any time, but I promise you before the night is over, you will have come to know me quite well. I will enlighten you further as the evening wanes; however, the night is short and we still have a lot to do. Remember this is only your first stop of the evening. This is a learn-as-you-go game and I think you've learned all that you can here. So when you are finished reveling in my creation of "The Man in the Chair," you may scroll to the next accept box, where you will receive your next set of instructions.

I know the scene I left you is fantastic, but don't indulge too long. Remember you are on a time limit. For now, I guess you can refer to me as "the Writer," or if you think I have true artistic ability in my work, perhaps the title of "the Artist" is more to your liking? Hah. Hear from you soon.

"What a complete nutjob," James said out loud. Who was this maniac? How did the Writer, as James would never refer to him or her as an artist, know about the dead man's fetish for child pornogra-

THE WRITER

phy? Just how many of these grotesque scenes were waiting for him in this game? What did the man in the chair have to do with himself? What was the purpose of being shown this horrid display? James didn't know the man in the chair from Adam. He had come here hoping for some answers but instead only received more questions. "This is the worst game ever," speaking aloud yet again.

Using the barrel of the pistol, he moved the mouse slightly and clicked *open*. A new address appeared on the screen.

> 919 Monteith Ave., Cincinnati, OH. You have 45 minutes. Remember, no one else is to be involved, but feel free to bring an extra hand. Lol, sorry, I just can't resist a hilarious pun. The countdown has begun.

James backed gradually out of the room, not wanting to turn his back on the one-handed, blind man. He did not believe in ghosts but did not like the idea of this room or anything in it, being where he couldn't see it.

There would be no problem finding the property, and he knew he could make it in forty-five minutes easily. He owned it too. Pondering on the way to the truck, how many properties could he possibly visit in a single evening? Not even a whole evening anymore. How many could there possibly be in the hours left? More than he wished there was going to be, that was for sure. He knew he was going to find out, albeit to his dislike. Back in the truck cab, the pistol was returned to the console and the motor started. En route he was to the next property.

Chapter 3

"Have you ever seen anything like this in all your years on the force?" Deputy Fore asked.

Sgt. Deke considered the question. "I've seen drive-by shootings that left victims looking like Swiss cheese. Bodies cut out of vehicles so disfigured even their own parents couldn't recognize them. I had a domestic call once where the husband had used a machete on his wife to play Whac-A-Mole before eating a shotgun blast himself. Got called to a scene where a technician who was doing service on an elevator had been smashed flat as a McDonald's pancake.

"In 2003 I seen what was left of a disgruntled employee who had tried sending a bomb to his boss but had accidently blown himself up instead. Blew off both arms, removed his face, and tore through his chest, leaving a lovely mess for his wife to find. And that's a quick few of a dirty dozen plus some I could tell you…but I've never seen anything like this. I haven't even seen anything like this in a movie. This is beyond overkill."

Deputy Fore, a rookie who thought he was meant to be an officer, having doubts about that now, was full of nervous energy. New to the force, he had not yet become as grizzled and numb like Sgt. Deke, who was not far from retiring. "Do you think this is the husband?" Again, Deke considered the question. What he was looking at, laying approximately four feet from the foot of the stairwell, was what remained of a human being. The body was so mutilated it was uncertain to tell if it had been male or female. From the waist down, everything looked the way a body is supposed to look. From the waist up, there was so much damage Deke couldn't make since of what his eyes were telling him.

THE WRITER

The ceilings were eighteen feet high in the room and had blood sprayed on them, as did the walls, along with chunks of tissue. Splintered bone and teeth were spread across the room and stuck in the wall like shrapnel. The marble floor of the entryway of the home, which housed the stairwell, was saturated with blood, making it impossible not to be totally avoided by deputies. What remained from the waist up looked like raw hamburger with tattered pieces of clothing minced in and bone fragments peppering a stew. Head, arms, hands, torso, organs, spinal cord, and ribs all destroyed. They had been chopped up, severed, cut, destroyed, mutilated—pick any word you like, and he still couldn't describe what he was seeing. The heart, lungs, liver, intestines, essentially everything that is supposed to be inside, had been pummeled to what was the equivalent of a red paste. *What instrument of destruction had caused this?* he pondered.

It was almost as if whoever had done this was trying to erase the individual from existence, Deke thought. They must have worn themselves out completely trying to do it. Or maybe, he wondered, had the approaching sirens caused the cease? Had they been that close to catching the killer in the act? Once Shelia was awake, he hoped she would at least be able to fill in some of the missing blanks for them. "I'm not quite sure how they're going to figure that out," Sgt. Deke answered. "Maybe they can dig enough teeth out of the floor and the wall, or soup through the mush and retrieve enough for a dental identification."

"How are we supposed to get him or her out of here?" Fore asked another question.

"A gurney's out," the sarge told him. To this, Fore laughed out loud. Perhaps more because of nervous tension from the situation than the joke itself, but nonetheless it caught the attention of deputy Jasper as he was coming through the foyer.

"I'm glad you can find this so funny, Fore. Maybe once we figure out who this person was, we'll let you break the news to their next of kin and you can all share a good laugh." Jasper scowled. Jasper, who had brass running through his veins, thought he was God's gift to the Clermont sheriff's department. Even if his father and his father before him had not been retired officers, which he never let anyone forget that they were, Jasper still would have thought that way. He always considered himself the smartest person in the room regardless of whoever else occupied it at the same time.

"Shut your piehole," Sgt. Deke told him. "Deputy Fore was just asking me how we're going to move what's left of whoever this was. Maybe I'll have you grab a scoop shovel and a bag and let you show him yourself." Deputy Fore bit his lip not to laugh.

"Freaking hilarious, Sergeant," Jasper replied, then exited quickly into the dining room around the corner.

"Forget about that prick," Deke addressed deputy Fore once more. "Not his fault, really, his father was a prick too, and my guess is, so was his grandfather. He probably hails from a long line of pricks." Sarge gave a small chuckle. Fore smiled and snickered at the double entendre but didn't laugh out loud this time.

Fore knew that Deke was just trying to lighten up the mood some, mostly for his sake, and that Sgt. Deke also used humor as a coping mechanism. Some people drank, some smoked, some used meds legal or otherwise, and some people did all the above. But Deke used comedy. Albeit, usually dark comedy. Maybe once he had been around longer, things of this magnitude would disturb him less, he certainly hoped so.

Sgt. Deke was actually a very serious officer most of the time; however, when things were not to his liking, discomfort set in, or in a situation like this where things were just unbelievable, then the humor came out. Deke noticed the look on Fore's face, and the lack of pigment. Usually a healthy shade was now almost white. Sensing the rookie needed something to help ease the gravity of the situation, he added. "Actually, I have seen something worse than this."

"I don't know how that's possible. What could you possibly have seen that's worse than this?"

"It was 1988. My wife and I had just started dating. She was the most beautiful girl I'd ever seen, totally out of my league, and I would have done anything to impress her. In fact, that's about the only chance someone like me had with someone like her. I had to do something to really get her interest. She could have her pick of any

THE WRITER

guy she wanted. How I got so lucky, I'll never know, but I thank God daily because she's still outta my league even today.

"Anyway I had to do something she would really love even if I hated it. So I got front row concert tickets to her favorite rock band. We were so close we were nearly on the stage ourselves. I even sprung for backstage passes. The evening started off fine. We were hitting it off well. The opening act was actually more to my liking than the headliner, but I didn't tell her that, of course. The crowd seemed to enjoy them as well, and no one was getting crazy obnoxious or out of hand, and I was thrilled just to be there with Kristie. I didn't care about either band to be honest. I would have gone to see New Kids on the Block if it meant I could be with her.

Eventually, the headliner came on, and that's when it happened. The most horrifying, terrible, god-awful thing I've ever seen or heard in my life. The memory of that night still haunts me to this day. Sometimes I wake in a cold sweat, trembling… The horror."

"What?" the rookie asked. "What was so awful it could possibly be worse than anything you've mentioned already, or worse than this blob of human goo before us here?"

Sarge paused a few seconds longer for dramatic affect. Finally, he let out a deep breath and said, "Bon Jovi. Man, that guy *sucks*."

To this response, Fore absolutely lost it, breaking out into hysterical laughter. Realizing he would not be able to contain himself, he pulled his hat down over his face and ran outside to the patrol car, not wanting to be seen by his peers laughing uncontrollably at such a horrendous scene. If anyone saw him hiding behind his hat running away, they would assume he had gotten sick or was going to be. They may even think he was puking in his hat, and that was okay with him. He was a rookie after all, and that would be accepted more easily than would a rookie standing at such a grim sight howling with laughter.

Safely inside the car, he howled like a madman. Perhaps not solely on what Deke had said but also the gravity of the situation, nerves, and genuine disbelief of what he'd just beheld inside James and Shelia Seaver's home. Emotions had to be released someway, and apparently, they were exiting in a fit of uncontrollable laughter.

Bon Jovi, he thought, bringing more hysteria. Deputy Fore then said out loud, "I know something worse than his singing." In a voice impersonating the sergeant, he answered back, "Nothing can be worse than that." Again, in his own voice, he said, "His acting." Finally, once more as the sarge, "Touché," which sent Fore into another fit of laughter.

Chapter 4

James arrived at the Monteith property with less time to spare then he initially anticipated. The traffic was not bad at this late hour, but the traffic lights at this time stay green on the main drags a lot longer than they do for the side streets, and he felt he must have caught at least 115 lights that took two years to turn green at every stop. Creating a hurry-up-and-wait mentality as he sat staring at the red lights, he tried to use the power of the force to change them with his mind, but to no avail. If only he were a Jedi, he mused.

He managed to arrive with about seven minutes to spare, so he had no time to waste finding the laptop that awaited him somewhere inside. Without hesitation, he went straight to the door and turned the knob, knowing it would not be locked. Even if it had been locked, the four-by-five glass window panes that lined the door frame on either side would have made access easy—just break out the glass and turn the dead bolt. They were supposed to be replaced months ago to window block. Why they were still here was unknown. Peterson could be a slacker at times.

James swung the door open and hollered inside not expecting to receive an answer, but what did greet him was a stench so fowl he almost choked. The smell engulfed him as he stepped inside. Opening the door was like opening a giant vent that was now drawing the smell that had been locked up inside, out. James grabbed his jacket and pulled it up over his nose to keep out as much of the odor as possible, but it still worked its way through the material. The repugnant air hung in the house like humidity did on a hot day. *Oh, I can't wait to see where that smells coming from*, he thought, certain the smell was related to death, no doubt. Wasn't that what this game was about, after all? Of course it was.

Inside the entryway, the living room was adjacent with no lights on. A light from an outside streetlamp shone through the front door that he would leave open to help suck out some of this foul smell, enough to illuminate the hallway. At the far end of the hall, a small glow coming from the kitchen appeared not to be a kitchen light on but rather one giving light from the basement and reflecting off the tiled backsplash over the sink. Someone who has never been here before would not have known the basement door was to the right of the kitchen entrance, but he did own the place.

Already having the 9mm in hand, he used it to turn on the switch for the hall light, which naturally did not come on. Most certainly, the only lights that worked in here were the ones left on for him, he gathered. Whatever was waiting for him to see at this location would be where that light was coming from.

On course to the basement, the smell grew much worse. The first stop had not smelled at all in the room with the man in the chair. Here, though not even finding what he had come for yet, the smell was almost unbearable already. If it was this bad up here, how bad would it be when he came upon the source? As he reached the top of the stairs, a series of three small beeps went off over his head. James almost pulled the trigger on the 9mm and his sphincter. "What the," he started. Then noted it was only the smoke alarm letting it be known the batteries needed changed. *Some Jedi I'd make*, he told himself. *A smoke alarm almost made me crap my pants.* A small laugh escaped him. Not willing to chance that happening again, he reached up and grabbed the smoke alarm which was hanging inside the basement stairwell ceiling, and removed the battery. The trash can at the top of the stairs became the new place for both after he deposited them there, then began his descent to the basement.

The basement was approximately 1,500 sq. ft. and unfinished. The smell coming from it, however, made it seem ten times that size. *I don't even want to find out what's in there*, he addressed himself. At the foot of the stairs was another door opened just enough so light could get through and shine into the upstairs kitchen, inviting James to come hither. This too had been done intentionally, as would be

THE WRITER

the case all night. This entire game, as the Writer called it, would be set up for him, having no delusions to the contrary. Using the pistol to open the door full swing, his breathing stopped as the creation that was left for him presented itself.

James looked on in pure shock at what was before him. Roughly ten feet inside the door, a man, what used to be a man, was stretched out with both arms over his head, each in their own set of handcuffs that were clamped around a gas line securely anchored to the joist. The man had been peeled of his skin from head to toe. His genitalia had been removed and were now protruding from his mouth, the testicles lying on his chin. Both left and right ductus deferens dangled down like spent, bloody, party popper streamers.

A pool of blood beneath the skinless nightmare flooded the ground. The floor drain had gotten clogged with fleshy tissue that had been discarded while the removing of flesh had occurred. *Where is the skin?* he wondered. A quick glance around the basement as he stood in place brought to his attention a washer and dryer to the far-right side. The washer drained into a double bowl concrete basin. Both bowls had filled and overflowed. Red water covered the front and sides of the basin, which had stained as it ran over into the puddle on the floor. Like small rivers of blood feeding into an ocean of gore atop the drain.

James had caught his breath again, but the taste that filled his mouth and nostrils made him wish he was still holding his breath. Breathing through his jacket wasn't cutting it, he thought, then added that was a poor choice of words under the circumstances. The skin—the skin must be in the washer. The Writer had whittled this man of his skin and put it in the washer, but why? *What significance was there in that?* he wondered. *And why was he fed his own cock 'n' balls?*

The laptop—where was the laptop? It had to be close. *Let me read the stupid email and get outta here.* Quickly scanning the room, he found it. Over in the corner, almost behind him, was a TV and couch with a laptop open on the coffee table between them, waiting for James to find it. He had not seen anything over that way as he had entered the room. All his attention had been drawn to the hanging corpse, followed immediately by questioning where the skin was.

Now not only did he see the laptop but also seen that a message waited, for him of course. The laptops had been facing him as he entered at every stop tonight. What a swell psychopath the Writer was. "Wonder who that's from," he asked out loud. Walking toward the table the laptop was on led him away from the pool of goo around the drain, so he didn't have to walk through it. That would make this just about perfect had he needed to drudge through that mess, he told himself.

Although anxious to get out of this house as soon as possible, he was also curious to find out what the man in the basement had done to deserve such a horrible death. He was confident the email would explain. He would receive answers, all right. Maybe not answers to the questions he had played this sadistic game for, but answers nonetheless. He was certain that the Writer could not resist the chance to explain the good deed he had served the world by creating this. As he reached the laptop, he leaned over to hit the *open* box with the mouse, no severed hand this time, and was met with a familiar greeting.

Third email:

> Hello, James… How's it hanging? Apologies, I just do so love a good pun. Apologies for the stench as well. I'm sure by this time "the man in the basement" must be mighty ripe. I hope that it is not too overwhelming for you. I bet you're asking yourself what he did to be deserving of such an awesome demise. Allow me to enlighten you.
>
> The skinless piñata was a pedophile. That, to me, is just about the worst thing someone could be. Anyone who could hurt a child in such a way is something I find intolerable. I'm sure you would agree the punishment for an individual who actually molests children versus one who watches pornography with children in it should be much more severe, would you not? Believe me when I tell you I took much pleasure and

as much time as I could to inflict all the hurt possible before he left this earth. It was a long, excruciating death, I assure you, and I relished every second of it. I only wish it could have lasted longer.

Suffice it to say, he was well aware of why he was tortured so. Oh, how he begged for mercy and forgiveness. Much, I imagine, the same way his underage victims begged and pleaded for the monster to stop raping them. As he failed to answer their cries and request for mercy, I too rejected his. As for forgiveness, I'm not in the forgiveness business, James. Me, I'm in the punishment phase of things. Only God is in the full-time forgiveness scene. I'm sure you're well aware I'm not God. You may think by now I'm the devil, but that is not the case either. I'm just someone seeking right for those who have been truly wronged. A hero for the wronged, you could say.

You may not agree with my sentencing, but I believe you could have little compassion for these men you are meeting tonight, thus far nor yet to come. You are probably aware that the skin is in the washer but unsure why. He was such a filthy, disgusting individual I thought he needed to be cleaned. Although I'm afraid I couldn't wash away his sins that way. Lol. Only Jesus can do that. Nor am I him either. But I gave it a shot. Originally, I'd thought of inserting the penis of "the man in the basement" into his anus, which is where he liked to insert it into, young boys mostly, though not solely restricted to; occasionally, the service of an underage girl would suffice. He did, however, have an oral fixation that he made his victims partake in that was second to nothing else, so I thought it more fitting to complete my art as such.

If you're wondering how I know all this, I can tell you some of it was research. A lot of it was also learned during our time in the basement together. It's amazing what people will confess to when they're being skinned alive. So now you know who I am. That may not be the answer you were hoping for, but it's the only one I have for the time being. Just a hero passing judgment.

Here are some answers that may be more to your liking. As of now, your wife is alive and, well, resting. Your daughter, as we both know, is in Australia. She will not be involved in any way tonight one way or the other in our game. You must think of me by now to be many things. Most likely, none of them are good. That said, I am sure you can theorize I would not hurt a child in any sort of way. I think you are well aware of my disgust toward the harm of a child. Even though yours is almost 18 now and soon will not be underage, she is still a child. Even if she was of age, she would not be a part of this. She does not have a purpose in what I've laid out for you.

How do I know of your daughter's age and location, you ask? Research I've been working on this evening, getting prepared for a long time. So are you ready to keep playing, James? Of course you are. You know how this works by now. I can't wait for you to see what's next. It is my personal favorite of the evening. So whenever you're ready…

James wanted to read the message again. Sometimes a second reading could help make more sense of things, but the stench of wasted life in the air was suffocating, and he just wanted out of here.

THE WRITER

He scrolled to accept and a third address, another property of his, naturally, lit up on screen.

421 Wyoming Ave… Twenty-five minutes

Taking a deep breath through his jacket sleeve, he held it in, spun around, and ran to the stairs, ascending two at a time, turned the corner in the kitchen, at last making a mad dash for the front door, pulling it shut on the way through. Outside, he finally exhaled. With both hands on hips, he drew in fresh, clean air, vanquishing the stale, dead oxygen that he had been inhaling for what seemed forever. Catching fresh breath as he walked to the truck still in disbelief at just what was taking place this nightmarish evening. Inside the cab once more, he housed the 9mm, shifted to reverse, and exited the driveway.

Twenty-five minutes to reflect on everything that was happening tonight. Even if he had twenty-five years, he didn't think he could figure out what was going on or why he had been chosen for this sick game in the first place. However, he didn't have twenty-five years; only twenty-five minutes. James drove, with hope of finding answers at the next address, making this place in the rearview mirror a horrible memory he would love to forget.

Chapter 5

The elevator on the north side of the Christ Hospital ascended to the third floor carrying the Writer. The Writer, who had gone by many names throughout his existence, was now using the alias Dolan, or as he liked to refer to himself on occasion, Rolling Dolan. Only he pronounced Rolling as Rollan, so the two rhymed together. Fitting, he thought, since he just kept right on rolling along.

Gaining entry to where he needed to get to in the hospital would not be a problem. Rollan Dolan had done his homework. He knew the routines and schedules of everyone he would have to encounter while he made his visit here tonight. He was also aware there would be a security guard posted outside Shelia's door. Not knowing who the victim at the house had been, or who the killer had been either, police decided it necessary to do as such. Whoever the killer was may have planned to kill Shelia too but had been interrupted by the approaching officers before they could finish.

Yes, Rollan Dolan had come prepared, already having mapped out the fastest way in and out with as little interference as possible. He knew some contact was unavoidable, but at this late hour, he knew it would be limited as well. Plus, dressed as a doctor, he had learned that very few questions would be raised. People take one look at the white lab coat and assume you're doing what you should be doing. Dr. Dolan had his fancy white coat and with it a pocket full of syringes filled with his homemade concoction for anyone that got in his way. He carried a taser as well, in case things got off way off course, but he was confident it wouldn't be needed. Nothing lethal, his mission tonight was not to kill or maim anyone, only to incapacitate those who would stand in his way of achieving what he had come for—Shelia.

THE WRITER

Shelia was on the third floor in room 310. After a thorough examination, all that had turned up was a small about of anesthetic and a tiny hole in her neck where the dose had been administered. All vitals were normal, no contusions or abrasions, no broken bones, and no signs of sexual assault were found either. It was as if someone had just put her to sleep and left her to be found. With all the testing and procedures finished, Shelia had been admitted to a private room to wait until she woke again. Maybe once she was coherent, she could enlighten them as to what took place. The police were hoping as much too.

The sheriff department had informed the hospital that no drugs or any paraphernalia had been discovered at the scene other than what was found on whoever had been destroyed in the entryway. The house was clean, except for the butchered body at the foot of the stairs, of course, and the mess that went along with that. They were made aware that an officer would be posted at her room until further notice, and they were to be notified immediately when she was conscious. They needed answers fast, and more lives could be at stake.

Now laying alone in her room, Shelia was oblivious to anything going on. Dr. Rollan Dolan was exiting the elevator to her floor. Approaching the nurses' station that was between himself and room 310, he said, "Good evening, nurse, I'm Dr. Dolan. Dr. Casey, in charge of the patient in room 310, asked if I'd check in on her for him on my way out to see if she was awake yet. It seems she is a matter of particular importance to the police and they want to be notified as soon as she wakes. I'm afraid he's indisposed at the moment." By indisposed, he meant the doctor had received a dose of one of his personal hypodermics and was sleeping it off in an industrial closet. "I told him I didn't mind. I was just going to go home to sleep. That was all anyway." Nurse Hopkins barely looked up from her computer screen to wave him on ahead.

"Sleep?" she asked. "What's that? I wish I knew what sleep was. I work twelve-hour shifts, sometimes double shifts, then when I get home, I have mouths to feed, laundry to wash, homework to help with, and dogs to take out. What's sleep?" Before Dolan had time to answer, "And do you think my husband can lift a finger to help?

Of course not, he's about as useless as vasectomized balls. And if he helped with any homework, the teacher would think my kids were complete morons who have parents that are siblings. Why do I stay with him, you ask? Because I don't have time for a divorce"—she took a look down the hall now to see if anyone else was in earshot, and added—"and he's great in bed."

Dolan, who had not uttered a word since she began her rant, was wishing he had just walked on by without speaking to her now. No doubt she would not have even bothered to speak, he thought. She's too self-indulged, vulgar, and brash as well. Qualities he very much disliked and most definitely did not approve of. *If sleep is what you seek, my miserable Rolly Polly, don't worry. You will be sleeping soundly in just a very short matter of moments*, thinking to himself.

Out loud, however, he smiled and told her that he would pray for her. At this, she looked up from her screen wide-eyed and taken aback, looking as though she had been smacked. "My apologies, I didn't mean to offend, it's been a long day" was her excuse. "No apology necessary, dear, I'll remember you in my prayers, and I'll ask that you may find time to get some sleep while I'm at it," he added as he gave a wink. *Not all prayers are answered*, he thought, caressing one of the syringes in his pocket. *But I have a good feeling about that one.*

Dolan had found that if a situation ever occurred you wished to get out of, all you had to do was inject religious belief into the conversation, and that usually shut people down. The majority of people did not wish to discuss Jesus, or God, heaven or hell. They didn't want to think about them. He found it sad, really, but it had benefitted his intentions on many occasions. Dolan believed in the trinity. He also believed wholeheartedly in the Bible, his favorite scripture being Exodus 21–24. "An eye for an eye, tooth for a tooth, hand for a hand, foot for a foot."

Unfortunately for Dolan, as well the many that suffered at his hand, according to verse, it was Old Testament scripture. Had he known how to read the Bible correctly, rightfully dividing the word of truth, he would have known as much. Not that it would have made a difference. No, he still would have been what he was regardless, a born killer who loved the hunt. Using scripture as he saw fit allowed him to justify in his twisted mind anything he did. Dolan was not proficient at biblical interpretation, but he was more than efficient at killing. Actually thinking of himself as doing God's work, vanquishing evil from the world, not seeing himself as an equal evil to those he abolished.

No, Dr. Rollan Dolan just kept on strollin'. And right now, he was strolling around the hallway corner and straight to room 310. Turning the corner, he saw the deputy outside of the room which hosted Shelia. The ever-vigilant officer was propped back in a chair leaning against the wall. Drawing closer, he could now hear the fat man snoring. *That's fantastic*, Dolan thought to himself. *This will actually take some of the thrill out of the game. Walking up on a sleeping fat man so deep in sleep he was probably dreaming, most likely about pies and cakes, from the looks of the portly beast. Putting a needle in his neck this way would be less fun for sure, but at least there was still nurse Hopkins to have a go with. Soon her sleep would come*, he mused.

Stepping over the outstretched feet of the officer, Dolan pulled the second syringe of the evening thus far and inserted it into the fatty meat around the collar and pushed the plunger through the barrel, injecting the cocktail into the sweat-soaked body. The stench of BO was barely covering the smell of scotch. Dolan had no doubt that a flask would be found somewhere on his person had he searched. Perhaps when the officer was found later, unconscious, his superiors would take notice. Drunk, carrying a flask, and the patient he was there to protect now missing would surely be cause enough for his dismissal from the force. Dr. Dolan thoroughly hoped so.

"Fat people disgust me," he said aloud. The officer was so inebriated he didn't even flinch when the needle pricked the skin. *What a waste*, Dolan thought. *Waste of a human being and needle both. Probably wasn't necessary to dope him up, but why take chances.*

Stepping into Shelia's room, he dropped the hypodermic into the hazardous container, then turned to face the bed. Now Nurse Hopkins's turn. Walking to the head of the bed, he paused a moment to admire her beauty before pushing the call button. "This is Nurse Hopkins, is everything okay in there, Doctor?"

"Yes, I think Mrs. Seavers may be waking up, could you come down here, please? And pay no attention to the officer passed out in the chair. He reeks of scotch. I'll ask you to call the police department to report him after you assist me with the patient."

"Right away, Doctor." Nurse Hopkins closed the page she was currently on in her laptop, which was a dating site. She was returning sex messages to horny married men looking to fool around. A nympho as well as vulgar, she was. Then she speed-walked down to room 310.

Entering the door, she saw Shelia in the bed but no Dr. Dolan. *Perhaps he stepped into the*—That was as far as her thought went before she was grabbed from behind, head pulled back, and a small sting touched her neck. She reached back over her shoulder, clawing at whoever was behind her, but only for a short moment. Unable to scream as her assailant was covering her mouth, she quickly succumbed to the cocktail Dr. Dolan had administered.

Mercy, she weighs as much as that fat cop in the hallway looks like he must weigh, Dolan thought as he was now holding her entire body weight. *Now this is more like it.* Attacking a live person was much more invigorating than dosing a drunken cop sleeping it off, even if he had snuck up from behind her to do so. Although he had no plans to kill her, the excitement was still there—the thrill of the pursuit, the feeling of power. It was addicting. Nothing in comparison to past deeds already completed and waiting for James to discover this evening. Those had been far more exceptional.

Holding her under the arms, he dragged her inside to the bathroom just across from the foot of the bed. Pulling her all the way inside, he dropped her onto the cold tile floor, vacated the bath, and pulled the door closed. Shelia began to stir, now speaking but making no sense. "The flow of honey taste sweet," she murmured. A smirk fell across Dolan's face. "You want something sweet, my dear? Sweets I have a plenty." Extracting a needle from the white coat, he removed the cap, raised it, flicked it thrice to bring the bubbles to surface and expel the air, then gently inserted the small stinger into a welcoming vein and released his cocktail. Doing so with a great deal of more care and consideration than he'd showed the fat cop and the profane nurse. He didn't want his prized possession harmed. That wouldn't do, at least not at this juncture.

Since she was semiconscious, there was no need to administer the entire syringe. After recapping it, he returned the tool to his pocket and unhooked Shelia from the monitors. As he lowered her bed to the flat position, she tried speaking once more but this time was inaudible completely. Dr. Dolan pushed the bed through the door into the hallway and toward the elevator, which was a mere ten feet down and across an intersecting hallway. No one saw him exit the room or push the elevator call button, enter the box, and descend to the first floor. The elevator was empty and played music to a song he knew but couldn't remember who it was by. It didn't matter; he hated the song and hoped thoroughly that it would not get stuck in his head now and stay there for the rest of the evening's festivities. What a downer that would be.

The bed rolled over the white tile with ease as Dr. Dolan steered from behind. Now only twenty feet lay between them and the exit where his personal vehicle was waiting. A brand-new Cadillac Escalade, complete with every option possible plus some he had added himself, including one very special custom accessory just for occasions such as tonight. A secret compartment, actually there were a few, but one in particular that he was most proud of was a compartment for hiding bodies. More often than not, it would be used for dead bodies, but not tonight. Tonight it would have a very special guest, one he needed alive and in pristine condition, and here she was almost delivered.

The SUV's back door opened upward like most do, as well the seats could be removed like factory models. There was the normal storage area under panels that could be pulled up, plus his had a false front that could be moved via remote control and folded down with the push of a button, giving access to a storage space big enough to hold not one but two bodies. Then, with a push of a button, the door closed tight again. Afterward, any number of things could be put into the rear factory storage unit, disguising it even further.

Another feature that made this model superior to the rest was that his customized box was soundproof. After all, if by chance a subject gained consciousness while inside and started screaming or kicking, that would be bad. What if he got pulled over or was in an accident and an officer were present when the stowaway was making all kind of noise? That would be even worse.

Finally, he had installed a camera linked to his phone with speakers so he could communicate with the inhabitants of the box should it be necessary. With the majority of the passengers being void of life, it would mostly be moot, but Dolan prided himself on always being prepared for anything and left little to chance.

Almost to the door now; one checkpoint left. Taking a patient from the hospital in the bed would no doubt draw unneeded attention, but he had that covered. At the desk just inside the door needed to exit where two individuals normally would be, sat only one. Security guard Mumford who was past retirement age was making his rounds, which left only the receptionist, Tina Calvert. She was even older than Mumford, if you can believe that, and was strictly no-nonsense. No doubt she would make trouble. Not wishing to hurt the poor elderly lady or using a needle, he opted for the good old reliable pull-the-fire-alarm move.

That should stir up enough commotion, even at this time of night, to sidetrack her long enough to wheel Shelia out to the soundproof pod that was waiting. If Tina fallowed protocol, and Dolan knew that she would, she would be too busy to notice the good doctor and the patient vacating the premises. If worse came to worse, he could easily share with her the rest of Shelia's unused portion from her needle. If it had to be done and all else failed to go as planned, he would simply snap her neck. There would be no enjoyment from it since she was 110 years old and her bones could break like twigs, but if it had to be done, so be it.

His fingers clasped the fire emergency alarm and pulled. The sound was deafening inside the cold fluorescent-lit hallway as it was reverberating off the concrete walls and floors, almost seeming to gain volume. At the desk, Mrs. Calvert was beside herself and so distraught she wouldn't have noticed Dolan or anyone else exiting the building as unusual, under the circumstances. Nonetheless, Dolan passed by her without haste, exited through the sliding doors, and rolled across the short span of driveway to his caddy. The back door

THE WRITER

rose as he approached the vehicle, and he hit the remote button to open the false front plate.

With the secret compartment now accessible, he carefully loaded his prize into the box. Dolan wanted not so much as a bruise nor scratch on his most valued possession. Securing the false door as well as the rear door, he walked to the front of his ride removing his white coat and got behind the wheel. A second stash compartment he'd created in the passenger side floorboard was opened. He quickly threw the white coat inside of it, as well as the fake hair he had been wearing. The prosthetic nose and fake mustache followed before the compartment was resealed.

Rollan Dolan turned the ignition key and the vehicle came to life. At once, the radio began to play. The last station he had been tuned to was now playing Bon Jovi. "Man, this guy sucks," he said out loud with complete and utter disgust, immediately changing the station. *Perhaps one day you'll take a ride in my special box*, he mused. *Do the world a favor for all the crimes you've committed against humanity. The least of which being "This House Is Not for Sale." What a piece of garbage. Not his biggest POS but still a solid turd. Oh, dear sweet Lord, don't even get me started on his acting. That in itself is worth a month of torture in my laboratory. He's no Axl Rose, that's for sure.*

The preset button he had selected instead was for yacht rock radio. Christopher Cross was singing "Sailing." Not his favorite Christopher Cross song but a very appropriate one for the occasion. After all, he was sailing all right. Rollan Dolan pulled his land barge out of the dock of the hospital and would soon be sailing through green pastures on his way to the game's final destination. Again, a smirk lit his face. As the escalade left the harbor, he pushed a button under the dashboard, another aftermarket modification. The vanity tag on the back of the vehicle turned, changing from DRDOLAN simply to ROLLAN.

*****

Deputy Fore had almost composed himself now, still sitting in his squad car when a knock on his window shot his heart into his throat. Rolling down the window, he asked, "Are you trying to make me crap myself? Holy."

"Have you got yourself together yet"?

"Yeah, sure, Sarge. As well as I can be, I guess."

"Good. We got another body, over on Slane Ave."

"Slane Ave. Fitting name, but that's not in our jurisdiction."

"I know. However, the person who owns that particular piece of property is the same individual who lives at this address. Officers responded to a 911 call there and found a vic in his office dead. Not just dead, both his eyes have been removed along with one of his hands."

"Oh, this is fan-freaking-tastic. What is going on tonight?" Fore asked.

"I don't know but my gut says we're just getting started."

"So because James owns both properties, are they assuming he's the killer instead of what's left on the floor inside?"

"I don't think so. Way I got it, a laptop was at the scene with an email addressed to someone named James. The vic's name was Tim."

"What was in the email?" Fore wanted to know. "I still don't get why they want us to go."

"They didn't relay the entire email or divulge much more info. Apparently this is a time-sensitive thing—a real sense of urgency is required. They want extra eyes at the scene from someone who's been here tonight, compare notes kind of thing. Apparently, our captain and Lieutenant Higgins of the Cincinnati police department are old academy buddies, and he offered us to go have a look. I got the order to go and take someone with me. So you know as much as I do. Now, do you wanna stop asking so many questions and come with me to get answers already? Or are you gonna make me go get that prick Jasper to assist?"

"Sorry, Sarge. Yes, I'm ready. Anything to get away from here. I mean no matter what we find when we get there, it can't be worse than this right?"

"Or Bon Jovi," Deke replied. Fore laughed but without hysterics this time. Walking back to his car, the sarge couldn't help but feel again that this night was just getting started. He also wondered if Fore's words (it can't be worse than this right?) would come back to haunt him before the evening was through.

Chapter 6

James's thoughts again went to Shelia. Was she conscious yet? Had she been able to tell the police anything at all? If so, would it help his situation or hinder it? Nothing but more questions. He didn't fear for Chae because he knew she was a million miles away, and he had no doubt at all that the Writer meant what he'd said about not harming children. Besides, wasn't that one of the points to this game so far? The harming of children was not tolerated by the Writer. Strange, he thought to himself, how so many questions there were he needed answered, yet somehow, he knew so many things that were fact without even a second thought.

James didn't think any harm would befall Shelia either. After all, she hadn't harmed any children in any way similar to that of the victims he'd found thus far. The Writer most definitely knew this as well. However, James was certain this maniac was nutty as a fruitcake, so he couldn't be 100 percent sure of it. He still felt that she was only being used as a pawn to force himself into this mad game of learn-as-you-go, the Writer had called it, which was rapidly growing to not be a game of learning anything that he'd hoped to learn at all but only what the Writer wanted him to learn. What a load.

Just two blocks away now was his next visit. Coming to a complete stop, he took a deep breath before continuing slowly. The house was just three driveways up on the right. The truck entered the blacktop driveway and came to a stop just a few feet shy of the front entrance. Knowing now he would not need the gun, he took it from the console anyway, tucked it into his belt, and exited the cab. Approaching the door, he had no fear anymore that he may potentially be locked out. Whatever waited inside was meant for him to find. The knob turned freely, and the door pushed open without hesitation.

There could be a dog, he thought. *No. Even if there had been one here previously, it would be gone now. Maybe killed as well.* He didn't know the Writer's feelings on dogs, but he had a feeling if any animal had been here, it would not have been left alone to alter in any way whatever macabre work was left for James to find. No, sir. That wouldn't do at all. Great time and effort, planning, and consideration had gone into his creations. He wouldn't allow anything that could potentially destroy what he'd created to be left in the house. That would make it null and void.

James again remembered Boo who had been half eaten by his own loyal dog. The Writer would never take a chance on something similar to happen. Not to his precious "art." No, the coast was clear of this, he was sure. Still reluctant to enter because of the rancid stench rather than any creature, he covered his nose and mouth again with his jacket and entered.

Inside, the light shone but dimly. He walked to the first room off from the hallway, which was being used as a billiards room. A nine-foot table with leather pockets, not one of the cheap ones where the balls rolled to the end of the table after a shot was dropped. Pearl diamond inlays adorned the wood between the pockets. Not a cheap table at all.

A bar was set up at the far end of the table and stocked with what looked mostly to be varying brands of tequila. Bar stools lined either mirrored wall along the long sides of the table, and a giant television hung on the wall the nearest to where James stood. *This must be where the majority of their time is spent*, he thought. Three tall circular tables lined the wall under the television that were littered with used ashtrays, empty bottles, and blue squares of cue chalk, each table having three tall barstool chairs apiece. One table had a mirror made into the center of it which also had several small straws, razor blades, and what looked to be about a kilo of white powder in a plastic-wrapped brick.

James guessed a kilo only because of what he'd seen from movies and television, not from experience. Surely, this had been set out by the Writer to show him something. *Who gets out a whole kilo at one time to party?* No sooner did he ask himself that question than Charlie

THE WRITER

Sheen came into his mind. *Yeah, well, sure. Charlie, of course*, he told himself, but this was not Charlie's house. This wasn't Hollywood. It was Cincinnati.

He was reminded of two cokeheads he knew from his bachelorhood that would do blow for days at a time. They partied harder than anyone he'd ever met. What was funny was the fact that regardless of how much they packed into their faces, they still held jobs—regular full-time jobs. One of them even used to run to and from work every day, with an eight-hour workday, in the middle hanging garage doors. They were the most responsible users he ever heard of. The complete opposite of what you imagined from two cokeheads. It was kind of funny.

Last he heard of them, they'd both got clean. One was a preacher now, and the other was running his own business instead of running to work. Though he wasn't a preacher, he too had started walking the Christian life. Good for them. Most people don't get off that merry-go-round, he supposed.

Certain this was left for him to find, it must be part of the story the Writer wished to tell. Realizing the place did not have the stench of death as the last place he visited, he lowered his coat and was able to breathe normally.

The next room up the hall was a kitchen, then a bathroom. Both were empty of anything that he had come here to find. Beyond that was a door that only led to the backyard, so he went back up the hallway and ascended the stairs that was inside the entryway opposite the billiard room. This particular house had no basement, only small dark dank cellar. James hoped to God whatever had been left here for him to find was upstairs and he would not have to go into any cellar.

At the top of the stairs, you could go left, which led to more rooms, or right to a small bathroom, just feet away from the landing. A quick look in the bathroom led to nothing he'd come here for. As he turned to head back the opposite direction, he noticed a dim glow coming from under a door, three rooms down the hall. Slowly putting one foot in front of the other, he reached what was being used as a living room. *Nothing living in here though, I'm sure of that*, he told himself. *Nothing will be living anywhere in this house.*

As he looked inside, he noticed the light was actually coming from a light pole outside and throwing light through the small space between the curtains. Not enough light shone into the room to make out anything much more than shadows. Stepping into the room, James reached out and flipped the wall switch. The ceiling light illuminated the room, showing bright and clearly what had been left for him.

James's eyes grew wide, his chin dropped, and his pulse froze. His mind could not grasp what his eyes were showing to it. It wasn't possible, yet here it was anyway, right in front of him. Standing there in complete disbelief, his brain finally started to make sense of and rationalize what it had been given to process.

Unlike the previous victims of the night which had been found alone, here there were two. Two men. Both of whom had their heads removed and sown back on backwards. Their arms and legs had been removed and sown back on but in reversed position. Now for legs they had arms, with hands for feet. And where arms should have been, legs were attached, with feet for hands.

Each torso plus the genitalia and buttocks had been turned so their backs were facing James as he entered the room. Their heads had been reapplied backwards and was facing James's direction; however, they were both looking up at the ceiling. Something was protruding from the mouths. As he continued to look and define this human jigsaw puzzle, he noticed that each victim had something protruding from their anus as well. They had been impaled. Paying closer attention to the pike, he realized they were cue sticks. No doubt taken from the billiard room downstairs.

One man was positioned on a couch, the other on a chair, both being held in place with the end of the cues wedged firmly into each piece of furniture. Almost as if they were having a conversation, their heads tilted back in laughter. Each held a cigarette between his toes, which was now used as a hand.

James could not tell if each man's appendages were his own or if they had been swapped out as well. The awful reconfiguration made James think of a Masters of the Universe toy he'd owned as a kid. Modulok was its name. The entire body could be assembled, disassembled, and reassembled any way you wished. It too came with two heads.

But this was no toy, and though they appeared to both be laughing, nothing was funny about it at all. He was certain, however, the Writer thought it was hilarious. These were actual human beings who had been robbed of all their dignity. Maybe that was the point.

Fortunately, the procedure, rather procedures, had not been performed here. A task such as this required a lot of time and would make an awful mess. Most assuredly, he started his creation while they were yet alive. James was certain of that, which would mean blood, and lots of it. These two were dissembled and reassembled somewhere else and then brought here for their performance. A twisted version of what they had once been left in this position, they now held to be mocked and their secrets revealed on a laptop somewhere close by.

Unable to see their genitalia as their backs were facing James, he had no doubt that both men no longer possessed their sex organs. Where they were, he didn't know or want to guess and hoped sincerely that the email left for him would not divulge that information. Unlikely, he knew.

He had seen enough. He was growing tired of all the mutilation and self-righteousness of the mad writer, who believed it was his place to carry out the executions of evil men. Everyone he'd seen tonight had been horrible, even evil, people, sure, but what gave him the right to do this? Why all the trouble of displaying them like this? He simply could have killed them. Why the show? Why?

Staring at the sculptures of mayhem, not wanting to see but unable to look away, he began to feel hate for the Writer now, a thorough hate and vile disgust. It had been there since the opening line of the very first email and had festered and grew all night.

As a God-fearing man, he had tried to negate it, but now it was almost all-consuming. And the smug arrogance with which the emails were written only fueled the hate and anger. The sensation for him to destroy was now starting to fuel his thoughts. "Get yourself under control," he told himself out loud. You can't lose it now. If you do, he wins.

Still unsure of what this game was meant for other than to punish him as he had seen it, if he let his emotions get the better of him or lost it now, what good would it be for Shelia? He had to find out what this was all about not just for her but the sake of his daughter as well.

Trying to calm himself, he looked away from the abomination, the real-life Modulok, drew a deep breath, said a short prayer, then started to look for the laptop. He did not want to read it. Did not want to know what these two men had done to deserve such indignity. He did not want to play the game any longer. Did not, did not, did not.

The instructions were perfectly clear though. Once the game was started, it had to be seen through. No ifs, ands, or buts. For the sake of his family, he would see it through, all the way. No matter what else was left for him to endure.

Contacting the police was not an option. This game was for him and him alone. Even if bringing someone else into the game hadn't been against the rules, he'd never do it anyway. Why give this maniac more potential victims? No, thanks.

James noticed that one of the men's hands, which was now a foot, was positioned so it appeared to be pointing. Following the direction the finger was pointing, James saw the laptop sitting on the fireplace mantle. *Nice touch*, he thought. A look at the second of the two men on the furniture, he saw his hand, now a foot as well, was pointing at something also.

This one pointed to the wall the doorway was in that he'd used to enter the room. He hadn't noticed it when he had come in. His attention had been drawn immediately to the human jigsaws. When he turned to see what the hand-foot was pointing at, he discovered a huge mural that took up the entire wall. Something commissioned by the human shishkabobs, perhaps. Yeah, right. These two probably made this while coked out of their minds. You'd have to be high to paint this.

What he saw had to be the tackiest painting he'd ever seen in his life. Both men were in the painting, each in front of separate vehicles, ones he was certain they owned in real life. Each man had a Glock in both hands, leaning back on the hoods of their vehicles. Both were painted favorably with giant muscle, bulk, and tone. Unlike their real selves which were 125 pounds of black eyes, skin, and bones.

Each man wore a gold necklace adorned with a razor blade and a straw tucked behind their ear. Hundred-dollar bills were falling from their pockets and blowing through the air. Both men had a naked woman lying on the car hood to the side of where they stood, legs spread to get a full view of the shaved beaver, with huge oversized breasts and hard nipples.

The Sun was out in the picture and was a huge smiling face, wearing sunglasses. Its glasses were being pulled down by the Sun's hands while whistling at the women and giving a wink. The vehicle's headlights were eyes and the grills were smiling mouths.

Though the sun was out and it was a bright beautiful day in the neighborhood, it was snowing. The snow was supposed to be cocaine, he automatically assumed, since it was falling into piles of powder rather than evenly across the landscape.

Apparently, the cocaine on the table downstairs, along with various other copious amounts of God-knew-what, had attributed to this blasphemy. Even through all the horror the evening had provided thus far, James laughed out loud.

"Maybe these guys deserved what happened to them, just for this painting alone." He laughed again. While he was laughing, he looked again at the painting and noticed the license plates. A plate on one car said *we're*, the other car's said *cool*. This brought on another laugh, almost doubling him over howling.

"This can't be for real. How much coke would you have to pack in your face to do this and think it was a good idea?"

As he was doubled over laughing, uncontrollably now, he noticed two candles lying on the floor, beneath the painting. They were on either side of the piece of crap mural.

What are these doing here? he wondered. *Were they lit to pay homage to the sacred Saint of Suck?* More laughter came. As he laughed, he looked up and saw two candle wall sconces hanging on each side of the mural. His laughter stopped as quickly as it had begun.

He no longer had to wonder what had happened to the men's cock or balls. The sconce on the left and the right were both void of candles. What was now in their places was a set of testicles and a penis in each sconce. The flaccid penises themselves were each inside the glass insert while the testicles themselves protruded from under it and dangled beneath their bases.

All of a sudden, nothing was funny again.

"Let me just read the email and get outta here," he told himself. Turning around, he walked over to the fireplace mantle and retrieved his email.

Fourth email:

> Hello, James. I know you must be getting frustrated and most likely beginning to think about quitting, but I know you can do it. I know you will see it through. I have faith in you, James. Before I tell you what these two did and how they suffered, let me assure you again that Shelia is fine. I know you want her to stay that way, so just remember the rules. One thing I can tell you that I think will make you feel better about things, James, is that after you finish here, you have only one more stop to make.
>
> Now...let's talk about these two miserable, now-in-hell, worthless souls. The mural alone is worth 100 deaths. I'm sure you can attest. But seriously...keeping in theme with the rest of the evening, these two men hunted children.
>
> These men were sex traffickers, James. They stole children, then moved them around so sexual deviants could use and abuse them any way they saw fit. Innocent children raped repeatedly and passed around, living an existence worse than anything you could imagine.
>
> Besides the horrific life they were forced to live themselves, think about the children's parents, families, friends, and all the suffered loss that was felt. Not knowing what happened. How

THE WRITER

many sleepless nights? All the blame and torment the parents put on themselves. How many parents and victims committed suicide rather than live with the despair and loss? How many children died or were beaten to death in the sex slave trade just by these 2 men here alone? All so these 2 wastes of lives could pretend to be gangsters, pack their faces with blow, abuse young women themselves, and create god-awful paintings.

How many lives ruined and in complete disarray? Hence, the symbolism of the art I made for you. They too have been taken apart as the lives they destroyed were torn apart, and have been reassembled in chaos like the lives are now in chaos of the victims and families they left behind. I think it's fitting as it can be.

Though it may not look like they suffered much, I can assure you it was so. The cue stick that was used for impaling was used over and over again on their insides. Thrusting and retreating, thrusting and retreating again and again, churning their innards into butter, as so many children were done by these men who stole their innocence.

How many times do you think their victims begged their captor to stop hurting them as they sought sexual delight? Hundreds, thousands? I can't tell you the answer to that, but I can tell you with great certainty that these men begged. Oh, how they begged and begged for me to stop. They pleaded and cried, telling me how very, very sorry they were. Do you know what, James? Just like the predators these men handed little children over to didn't listen or stop the abuse, neither did I. I took great solace in their pain and suffering. It filled me with great pleasure and extreme delight to do unto them what they had allowed done to others. My only regret is that the time the three of us shared together could not have lasted much, much longer.

You did not know what these men were up to, I realize that. As well, you didn't have a clue as to the others you visited this evening, but they all live, rather I should say they did live, at your properties, James. And whether you knew or not, I feel you share some of the blame. You allowed these men occupancy in your residences, unwittingly allowing these tragedies to occur. Now it is up to me to invoke what I deem the necessary punishment. You will find out soon enough. You know what to do next. I'll allow you a full hour this time.

Standing there in disbelief, he no longer wanted to even think anymore. Sure, they rented from him, but he had nothing to do with anything that they did with their lives. In fact, he avoided everything he possibly could about his tenants and even the properties themselves for that matter. That's one reason he had a property manager, to avoid all contact. He didn't want to be bothered with anything involving the properties. Period.

Feeling completely spent, he scrolled down to the accept icon, and the final address appeared. As he read the address, a rage began to fill him. Anger, hatred, and bitterness were rising inside him, soon to boil over. It fueled him with a new desire. One he'd not felt until now but was surely becoming all-encompassing. The need, the desire, and want to kill. To end this madness and the monster who had taunted him this entire evening. A lust for revenge and to terminate this demon as soon as possible was now taking control.

James read the address once more. Not to remember it but only to help fuel the flame of the anger and hate that he felt, to feed it and make it grow. He would have no problem remembering the address anyway. It was his own.

Chapter 7

Sgt. Deke and Deputy Fore arrived at Slane Ave., parked their vehicles, and headed to the front door. The scene was not yet disturbed by EMTs. No need to rush them in. After all, the tenant was already deceased, and no amount of training would bring him back. Fore and Deke were greeted at the door by Lt. Higgins, who was in charge of the crime scene. After a brief introduction, the lieutenant led them to the man in the chair.

"What the" was as far as Fore got before being interrupted.

"So do we know if the eyes and hand are looking and pointing at the police, letting us know he sees us?" Deke asked the lieutenant.

Higgins responded, "That's what we thought too when we first came in, but after we discovered the email, addressed to James, we think now it's more of a display set up to let the victim know he had been seen. As well as maybe to let James know he was seen. Let me show you the email. Maybe there's something in it that is prudent to the crime scene you just came from. After you read the email, you'll discover this is a time-sensitive case. That's why we are doing things a little different here than usual. We got to move fast. We don't know who wrote the email. We're simply referring to them now as the Writer."

"The Writer?" Fore asked.

"After you read the message, you'll understand. It was that or the artist, and I refuse to call what he's done here art. Just read."

As the three men went to the desk, they passed by two more officers that did not exchange pleasantries. The big city police thought little of small-town hick interference and didn't think they would be of as much help as they would be in the way. However, the lieutenant had already forewarned them to play nice. This is not the way he wanted to do things either, but under the circumstances and the time restraints, he would take any help from them he could. Higgins opened the email and allowed Deke and Fore to read. "What a complete nut bar," Fore told them after he finished reading.

"Sounds to me like there's a previous email or some form of communication already taken place." Deke looked at Higgins to get a response.

"Has to be, and we're sure the next address the email mentions, there will be another message with more directions as well as another body or bodies."

"I'm sure you've already sent someone to that address."

"Yes, they should be there any minute now. Your captain assured me no emails or messages of any kind had been found at James's place?"

"Not unless something has been found since we left. I'll make a call, see who's still there, take another look. Deputy Jasper will still be there. I'm sure he'd be more than thrilled to know he was doing a favor for the big city boys in blue."

As if he knew they were speaking about him, Deke's phone rang. The name on the phone said Prick, which is how Deke had saved Jasper's name to his contact list. "Speak of the devil," he said before he answered the phone, and almost said "what's up, Prick" before catching himself. Deke put him on speaker. "Jasper, you're on speaker. Lt. Higgins from Cincinnati police department is with us. What you got?"

"Initially, as you know, we didn't look on the computers. However after Lt. Higgins spoke to us earlier about the laptop they had found with a message, I decided to see what we could find here. I found something interesting."

"What did you find?" Higgins asked abruptly.

"The Seaverses have a guesthouse."

"A guesthouse? All I seen was a garage that was bigger than a house, filled with expensive toys," Deke spoke.

"Correct, Sarge. The property here though is vast, and the house is not within viewing distance from the main house. It's on the other side of the property. I found a folder on the laptop marked guesthouse. When I opened it, there was a to-do list and a file for rent payments."

"They rent out the guesthouse?" Fore finally chimed in.

"Yes, but not full-time. It appears the house is rented out to hunters that come in from out of state during hunting season. Only staying a few days generally."

"Mother of God," Fore replied. "That could open the suspect pool to hunters all over the country."

"That's if it was a hunter. We don't even know that for sure."

"How long before we know anything about guesthouse?" Sarge reentered the conversation.

"I'm here now. No signs of forced entry. No bodies. But someone left here not long ago. The shower is still wet, and there's a pile of blood-soaked clothes with shoes inside the back door. Not just some blood either, a lot of it. The kind of blood one would expect to find from someone who had just left the main house after pulverizing whoever had been there."

Higgins, who had been taking all this in, finally contributed again, "Great work, Deputy Jasper. What else have you found? Have you found a laptop or a computer at the guesthouse yet? If so, is there anything on it we need to know about?

"Oh yeah, there's a laptop all right. And I'm sure it has portent information you will be interested in."

"Great work." Higgins told him. "We'll send you an email address so you can forward it to us."

"Sure thing."

Higgins sent the address of the man in the chair's laptop to Jasper and received the mail almost immediately. "We got it. Thanks, Deputy. Is there anything else you can tell us that you found there that is prudent?"

"The garage is empty. There could have been a vehicle inside. Whoever came here and showered could have wheels. That's about all I can give you right now. I'll keep digging around, and if I come across anything, I'll contact the sarge asap."

"Fantastic, Deputy. You do that."

"You got it, sir, and might I add what a privilege it is—" Sergeant Deke hung up the phone before Jasper had a chance to brownnose any further. Now all three men gathered around the laptop to read the newly attained email, as well as the three officers who had still not spoken to them since they had arrived. Higgins opened the mail, and each man read at his own pace until finishing the entire message. As each finished reading, they contemplated many things while each waited for Higgins to speak first.

"Okay. We have the first two emails, and it looks like a third will be waiting at the Monteith address." The three officers that were there when Deke and Fore entered the room excused themselves, leaving Deke, Fore, and Higgins alone once again.

Fore responded, "I have a question. The email told James not to involve anyone else or he couldn't promise Shelia would be okay. Yet here we are, involved up to our eyeballs. Does anyone think maybe this nut bar knows we're already involved and maybe Shelia is in danger? That is what he said, correct?"

"Yeah," Sarge spoke. "But James didn't involve us himself. Not wittingly at least. Unless of course he's purposely not erasing these emails so we would find them and be brought into the game without him reaching out on his own. Luckily for us, the Writer hadn't told him to erase the messages before continuing to the next address. Maybe we stumbled across his first mistake?"

"Maybe the Writer didn't tell him to delete them because he wanted James to leave them for us to find," Higgins answered. "I'm actually surprised he didn't tell James to leave the emails open as one of the rules so they would definitely be found. I'm sure he wants as many people as possible to view his so-called art. Perhaps James left them on purpose, or maybe he was in such a hurry to get out of where he was he didn't think about it. We only know for sure that almost two hours have passed since someone called from a burner phone and gave this address stating a man was dead in the house. My guess is that it wasn't James. Smart money says it was the Writer himself. He probably waited long enough to give James time to get some distance between he and us, then called it in."

THE WRITER

"One thing I'm sure of, this psycho isn't dumb, and I doubt he made a mistake. This has been thought out and methodical. And we haven't even got the third email yet. Who knows what we may find next or how many more messages after Monteith?"

"No, I don't think it's a mistake, not yet, not so early in the game anyway. It doesn't matter. We're involved regardless, and there's an officer at the hospital with Shelia. So let's shut up and get over there."

"Did you say you already had men there?" Fore asked Higgins.

"They should be any moment. We've got what we can here. I want to beat it to Monteith. The sooner the better." Higgins addressed one of his own officers and ordered him to stay behind and wait for the coroner, then motioned to Fore and the sarge to come with him.

"Our captain said aid you and follow orders until further notice. Lead the way," Deke replied.

Chapter 8

Rollan Dolan was indeed rolling, rolling right on along. "Over the river and through the woods to Seaverses' house we go," singing to himself as he rolled. The radio was still tuned to yacht rock radio, but he was not listening. He was too busy reminiscing about all the fun he'd had over the last several weeks getting things ready for this very night. All the stocking, planning, butchering, torture, the thrill of the hunt, all the sweat and anticipation, making sure every game piece was precisely how it should be, finally all coming to fruition. He was quite pleased and patting himself on the back. *Perhaps a clap from a cold clammy hand removed from the man in the chair.* He amused himself.

Yes, he had thought of everything. There would be no surprises for him tonight. Only the satisfaction of a job well done, or rather a game well played. Oh, how he wished he could see James's and the officers' faces when his art was found. He imagined what they would say to each other and wondered what they would say about him. What names they may call him. "Why would someone do this?" they would ask. "He must be crazy," they would say. Not knowing he was as sane as they were and doing the same thing they were doing. Defenders of justice were they all.

The very best part of the entire game was the torture. It always was. Oh, such sweet pleasure their cries brought him. Cutting out eyes, sawing off limbs, the peeling of flesh, all started with each victim still alive. Yes, the flesh, he relished. Skinning the man in the basement was so much fun he had not wanted it to end. The wretched pedophile was so much fun to punish. He didn't survive until the end, but Dolan had dragged it out as long as possible. Surely, the pervert would have lasted longer had Dolan not removed his man-

THE WRITER

hood with a straight razor and inserted it into his mouth, inflicting as much pain as possible in doing so. The man in the basement had penetrated so many young boys, destroying rectal cavities and tissue as well their innocence and youth. How satisfying it was to pay it all back to him with interest.

The song changed on the radio to one of his favorites, but so entrenched now in nostalgia was he that he didn't even notice. Dolan began to go back in his mind and relive the splendor of the man in the chair.

Dolan had been waiting in the living room closet which was directly behind the desk where the child pornography addict, soon to be known as the man in the chair, would be watching his filth. Dolan had put himself in the closet more than once and made the short walk across the room to make sure there were no squeaks from the closet door hinges nor in the floor. Both checked out fine. This would be so easy.

He sat patiently at the kitchen table, eating an apple from the fruit bowl that set atop it, waiting on the tenant to return home, refusing to sit on anything in the living room for fear of what bodily fluids may be on the furniture. Chewing his apple and humming a tune that was stuck in his head from the ride over, he waited for the sound of the man's car entering the driveway.

Just as Dolan stood to toss the apple into the trash can, he heard the engine of a car pulling in. After he deposited the core into the trash bin, Dolan casually walked to the closet and stepped inside. He wasn't sure how long he'd have to wait, but he was confident it would not be long. The tenant entered the house, dropped keys on the table, and turned on the light to the living room. If he came to the closet first to hang up anything, Dolan would spring and inject him there, but he was so hoping the tenant would be in his chair about to start his masturbating session so he could surprise him. Instead of getting the pleasure and satisfaction he desired, he would instead receive quite the opposite. Pain, regret, sorrow, and agony would take its place, at the hands of the vindicator.

The tenant did not go to the closet; instead, he went through the entryway up the hall and into the kitchen. Dolan heard the fridge open and heard a bottle cap twist off. Surely one of the beers that he had seen as he snooped through the house. Next, Dolan heard the toilet seat hit the porcelain tank, and a long fart escaped while the man relieved himself of urine. *That sounds runny*, Dolan thought and was delighted even more that he would be killing him soon. Not more than a minute passed before the man in the chair entered the room buck naked and sat in his favorite chair. The screen lit up, and after a few moments at the laptop and with a few clicks of the mouse, the screen changed to a scene of underage children about to participate in sex acts. Dolan refused to watch the screen any further. He looked only long enough to make sure that child porn was indeed on when he would end the sick bastard's good time.

The man in the chair was now groping himself with one hand as the other stayed on the mouse. After Dolan was certain the man was completely focused on his entertainment, he slowly turned the door knob and exited. Walking toward the desk, the syringe was already drawn he could hear the sounds now of one of the children. The volume was turned so low he hadn't noticed it from the closet. His anger deepened, and if he had not been in such control of himself, he would have attacked right then and beat the man to a pulp, but that would not do. That would ruin his game plan and he could not deviate from that.

The man in the chair said something now, but not to Dolan. No, he was talking dirty to the screen. Talking to the barely teenage girl on the screen, telling her she liked it and that he liked her and he wanted to—that was as far as he got. Dolan had wanted to wait until he thought the man was almost at climax and end his good time there, but he had had enough. Dolan wanted this man dead sooner than later. With his left arm, Dolan reached out and grabbed the man by the hair and lifted him up out of the chair, pulled him close, then head locked him with the same arm all in one swift moment so fast it almost couldn't be seen. The man was so surprised and scared he defecated all over the back of his legs and into the chair. Luckily, the chair blocked the feces from hitting Dolan himself, or his death would have been even worse.

THE WRITER

Dolan squeezed his neck so hard he crushed the wind pipe and cracked two vertebrates. Then he released the pressure just enough so the man in the chair would hear and understand what he was about to be told. "The death you are about to receive, you are not worthy of. You deserve much more than what I have allotted time for. You're lucky I need you as a teaching piece in this game, thus you will be treated as such. Otherwise, had circumstances been different, you would have suffered long and hard. Dolan again applied pressure and heard another crack, then letting go slightly, he thrust the needle up and drove it through the base of his skull and into the brain. With the needle in place, Dolan grabbed the man's right hand (the very one to soon be severed) the man had been flailing at him with to no avail whatsoever, squeezed it hard enough to break three bones inside, and used it to push the plunger, delivering the homemade cocktail Dolan had created into his brain.

Oh, how he wished that he could do things differently now with this individual, but he had an agenda and a plan in place. And he could not deviate from that. Regardless of how much he wanted to. Dolan let go, dropping the man into his own pile of waste and spun the chair around so the victim could see the face of his killer before he died, which would only be mere moments. Dolan stared into his dying face but said nothing else. Only watching until the final breath was taken.

After he was certain the man would no longer make such a bloody mess with the heart no longer beating, Dolan retrieved his tool bag from the closet. First, he removed the eyes and displayed them atop the monitor, after which he removed the hand and positioned it for his purpose. How amazing and thoroughly enthralling it had all been. He wished he could have done more, but he knew he had to stick to the script. Besides, this would be the first stop for James when the big evening came, and he felt he should start off slow and build up the mayhem as the night progressed. You don't want to start too big and go down from there. There was a method to the madness after all. And he had abided by it.

Dolan began whistling again as he spun the man in the chair back around to face the screen, pushed the chair in, and double-checked the eyes and hand were where and how he wanted them. Mercy, how satisfying it all had been. Dolan, who had never done a drug in his life except over-the-counter medications, could not imagine any narcotic in the world that could come close to making him feel the way he felt while he was administering agony.

The man in the chair had been a lot of fun indeed but was not his favorite victim. Or board game pieces, as he liked to think of them. No, that honor went to the man in the basement. Though he too died quicker than what Dolan had liked, he was meant to serve a purpose in the game as well, thus preventing Dolan from doing what he would have done under regular circumstances. Still, he had suffered and begged dearly, which was sweet music to Dolan's ears.

Music Dolan thought and was brought out of his trip down memory lane, realizing the station was playing a particular song he didn't care much for. It wasn't as detestable as Bon Jovi—nothing much was—but still a song he didn't care to hear. Instead of changing to find something more to his liking, he chose to lower the volume almost entirely. With it being nothing more now than a faint background sound, he returned to his memories of the man in the basement.

Again, Dolan lay in waiting for the second board piece, aka the man in the basement, to arrive home, sitting at a table in the basement. No bowl of fruit this time. The electric panel box was in the basement, which made this so convenient it was almost too easy. "Never look a gift horse in the mouth," his father used to tell him. His father was a complete nut bar. Borderline schizophrenic and obsessive-compulsive, but he was a certified genius. He had an IQ off the charts, with almost no common sense whatsoever. Dolan loved the old man and missed him dearly. *Enough of that*, he told himself. *You're getting off the subject… Back to what you were thinking about, dip-dingle.*

Flipping the desired breakers would allow the man to have light to see to get into the house, but once inside, he would find multiple things not working and bring him downstairs to check the breaker box. If you had a clueless tenant that knew absolutely nothing about electricity, they would immediately call the maintenance line. This tenant, however, was an electrician by trade, which left very little doubt that he himself would go downstairs to evaluate the problem, bringing him straight to where Dolan would be waiting.

The basement had an access door to the outside but had been screwed shut from the inside by the tenant himself. That left no chance of him entering that way. In the door was a smaller doggy door which had been covered over and screwed to the main door, but it had been screwed on from the outside. *What a genius.* Dolan laughed. Sometimes things just fell into place for him so perfectly it was as if someone wanted him to kill these individuals. A guiding hand perhaps, or a little gift for the avenging angel. He liked the sound of that one the best.

All he had to do was unscrew the plywood cover and crawl through. After he took the screws out that had been added to keep the main door closed from the inside, he simply stepped through the doorway and screwed the plywood back on before stepping back inside and pulling the door tight behind. Finally, he went over to the table and began laying out his instruments for the evening's festivities. Oh, what a night it was going to be. He had so many great and fantastic things planned for his guest.

Dolan rarely participated in sex. Relationships only made what he considered to be his calling more difficult. He could not be tied down to any one person. Besides, he found sex messy and felt it was overrated. Call him old-fashioned, but he wasn't into one-night stands or picking up strange women, and the thought of a prostitute sickened him. How someone could pay for something that countless others had already paid for and done God knew what with, he would never understand. Maybe some people had to pay for it, he assumed.

On those rare occasions he did engage in intercourse, it pertained to serve a purpose for the greater good of whatever game he was playing and who was being hunted. Besides, the lower profile he kept and the less people he associated with, the better off he was.

The closet he came to sexual gratification was when he was alone with his prey using his tools to slice and deliver sweet sorrow. Many times, over the course of years since his career started, he had become aroused during his pregame ritual of laying out the instruments of demise as he was doing now, and on more than one occasion had actually climaxed as the cutting had come to fruition. But never had he raped a single victim or even so much as had the thought of doing so. That went against his morals. Dolan was caressing his tools of sorrow and becoming aroused when he heard footsteps enter the house overhead.

The soon to be referred to as the man in the basement flipped the light switch, but no light came on. Dolan heard the man swearing as he walked to the switch in the hallway, flipped it, and still got no light. More cursing ensued. Dolan's heart thumped in his chest double time now. He felt like a kid at Christmas and it was almost time to open his present, literally. *So soon now*, he thought, and a smile lit up his face.

Having a conversation in his head, he thought, *Come on down, you're the next contestant on* The Price Is Right. *Oops, wrong game. You're the next contestant on* Who Wants to Die A Horribly Slow and Painful Death? *I do said the man who could get no lights to come on upstairs and was swearing as he went room to room turning on switches. Okay, okay, that's enough*, he told himself. *Get your game face on. He'll be coming down any moment.*

Just then, the doorway to the basement opened, and the tenant began his final descent to a place he'd never return from alive. Still swearing as he came. Obscenities strung together, making little or no sense at all. *This guy is an idiot*, Dolan thought. *His parents were probably brother and sister*. The door at the foot of the stairs opened now, and the next game piece stepped into near complete darkness. Dolan counted on the man to have his phone out using the flashlight and was correct. Luckily for Dolan, no one was on the phone at that time having a conversation with his trophy.

The table with Dolan's toys was around a corner in the opposite direction of the breaker box, waiting to be used. Almost half the basement was finished, which gave Dolan several places to hide. About five feet before you reached the breaker box was a door leading to a basement bathroom. Dolan stood just inside the bathroom door waiting for his present to pass. Dolan listened to the man swearing as he made his way across the darkened room until he passed the doorway in which Dolan was eagerly lurking. He heard the metal box open and stepped out quickly, not making a sound, placing himself directly behind his victim.

The breakers made a loud clicking sound as they were turned back on. Every light in the basement was now giving light. Dolan had made sure they would all turn on as the breaker was thrown. He wanted the man in the basement to see everything that was about to happen very clearly. After the lights were on, the tenant turned the light off on his phone, shut the panel door, then finally turned around. Dolan was standing directly in front of him now. The man jumped back so hard he hit the wall behind him. A scream began its escape but was silenced before it could get out. Dolan had grabbed ahold of his throat and cut off the air so fast that the man hadn't even seen his arm move.

Squeezing with his left hand, Dolan pulled the man to him spinning him a full 180 as he did so. Now the man was in a death grip, pressed tightly against Dolan. Dolan twisted the man's head upward, still holding his throat so he could look up into the eyes of his stalker. "The death you are soon to receive is too good for you, but I will do my best to make it as painful as possible. Enjoy the next few moments of consciousness. They will be the best of the rest of your life. When you awaken, you will receive more sorrow, torture, agony, and pain than you knew was possible."

The man in the bear hug was so frightened and so surprised he had hardly moved the entire time or even tried to fight back. He was frozen, almost catatonic. The whole ambush had only taken seconds, and he still wasn't sure what was happening. With his free right hand, Dolan delivered the syringe directly into the jugular vein. Unlike he had done with the man in the chair, this time he sent the plunger home himself. A different poison was administered as well. This one was not to kill but to incapacitate.

Different situations meant different circumstances. The first game piece was meant for a specific purpose and needed to be dealt with accordingly. Thus, Dolan had made a special homemade cocktail specifically for him, killing him almost immediately, which had not allowed him enough one-on-one time like usual. This individual was also meant for a specific purpose in the game, one that didn't call for death by needle as before. Nope. This time Dolan would get some quality time. Time he so desperately yearned for. Yes, this time he could play.

The man in the basement opened his eyes slowly and tried shaking away the blurry vision. Unsuccessful at first, but it did eventually clear. Had he known what lay in store, he would not have tried so hard to regain consciousness. Usually, people awake from nightmares into the real world where they're safe. He would be waking from his dream world into a living nightmare. In front of him was his card table, which had been pulled away from its usual place, and now instead of cards, chips, and ashtrays, it was adorned with tools of which he wanted no part of.

Trying to run, the board piece found he could not do so, nor could his scream escape. His mind was becoming aware now and starting to grasp the gravity of the situation. His mouth was gagged. His arms and legs were stretched out and bound. His hands were each in a handcuff with the other cuff clasped around the black iron gas line that fed the furnace and water heater over his head. His feet were shackled. Each one was stretched out tight and bolted to the floor with a concrete anchor that Dolan had installed while he was knocked out. The man was in a vertical position at the mercy of whoever had hung him here, and if that wasn't scary enough, he had been stripped completely naked.

As he ran in place hoping to break free, Dolan moved away from where he was watching and into the view of the fly stuck in his web. Finally, the man caught notice of his captor. "Try as you might, but you will be going nowhere this evening or ever again for that matter, other than to hell, I'm afraid." Dolan told him as he smiled. "I'm sure your master is waiting for you, now giddy and anticipating your arrival into eternal damnation, but he will have to wait his turn. I get first dibs."

With that, Dolan walked over to the table and picked up a straight razor, the first toy of the evening, then strolled over to the pedophile. Though it was useless to do so, still he kicked and flailed what little movement he had, which was very little, Dolan had made positive. "I've been waiting patiently for you for some time. Now we can finally play." Leaving the table of fun behind him, Dolan said nothing more with words for a long time. He would instead let his instruments do his talking for him.

The sexual deviant in the web was trying to scream with no real sound escaping; however, his bowels did let go. The stench was bad, but it would be a lot worse before the night was finished. Dolan knew from plenty years of experience. As he grabbed the man by the back of the head in his left hand and drew him close, with the right he touched the edge of the long straight razor to the side of the child molester's face. The bloodletting was about to begin.

Just above the left temple next to the hairline, Dolan applied pressure with the blade and cut a line down the cheek, over the jaw line, under the chin, back up the other side of the face, and across the forehead connecting the incision to where it started. The screams were muffled, but the blood came. Dolan leaned in and drew a long breath, savoring the smell of the crimson flow.

Behind the gag, words of repentance tried to escape but went unheard. Even through the gag, Dolan understood what was being said but did not heed their call.

The face had been cut and was ready to be peeled, but the time for that would be later. Starting with such an epic intro could send this game piece into shock, bringing his playtime to a screeching halt, and that would not do. He would save that for later, much later. Dolan intended to enjoy this thoroughly, and he had plenty of things planned before this night reached its climax.

For this reason, the incision over the eyes he'd purposely made shallow and more for the effect. He did not want a lot of blood running into his eyes and blurring his vision while he went to work on the body with his toys of fun. He wanted the man to see as much as possible of what lay in store for him.

Returning the blade to the table, he picked up a pair of needle-nose pliers. Slowly, he began removing toenails before trading the pliers for a hammer and smashing said toes one at a time. Reciting the, "This Little Piggy" rhyme as he went. After the hammer had served its purpose, Dolan once again chose a blade, albeit one of another sort this time. One more suited for what came next. The man in the basement was a canvas, and the artist was going to create a masterpiece.

Back in the SUV, Rollan Dolan smirked, recalling to himself the next three hours of torture he had inflicted on the molester—the cutting, dissecting, taunting, peeling, ripping, the disemboweling—how completely satisfying it all had been. As he drove toward his destination, he relived every moment the two had spent together. And he loved it.

Dolan believed there should be no such thing as a repeat sex offender and could not understand how a thing like that could even be allowed to happen. It was his opinion that all sex crimes primarily but not solely exclusive to children should be cause for immediate death. He wished he could kill them all. Though he knew that was completely out of the realm of possibility, he had made sure absolutely beyond a shadow of a doubt that this individual would not be a repeat offender. In Dolan's court of justice, there was no chance of it. Not ever.

Too many bleeding hearts, however, would not allow for such measures in a court of law, which is one reason why he had taken it upon himself to invoke punishment and true justice any chance he got. Not simply by just eliminating them, however. That would be too good for them. And besides, any moron could kill. What he did was make them pay and make them truly sorry and remorseful of their crimes. By the time he finished with his victims, not just the ones in this game, they had all been sorry. More sorry than any time in a cell could accomplish. After serving their useless sentence where good tax dollars were spent housing them, they would be released once more to prey on the public. The way his sentence was passed down, that was impossible.

Just before the man in the basement was going to lose consciousness for the last time, Dolan decided he should hurry and bring this trial to a close regardless of how much fun he was having. The man would be dead very shortly anyway, and Dolan could not let his grand finale be missed. Slapping the man to get his full attention as

THE WRITER

he was teetering on blackout, Dolan used the knife he'd started with that evening and cut the incision over the eyes deeper now.

"Just like ripping off a Band-Aid," Dolan said. "Only I'm quite positive this will hurt, a lot," he added. Then Dolan dug his nails in under the cut flesh below the hairline with each hand, until his fingers were in to their second knuckles, closed his thumbs tight and tore down in a quick ripping motion. The face tore from its owner with a sound that was music to his ears. The man in chains made no sound at all now, only convulsed and shook where he hung. Some of the skin had lacerated with small chunks of meat still intact where his lips had been, but for the most part, the face had peeled whole in one piece.

"No, no, no, you can't go yet. I have one more thing for you before you expire." Dolan grabbed the newest sharpest knife, one he'd not used yet and was saving for this moment. Reaching down, he grabbed the man's testicles and penis, and with a quick slice removed them from their owner. The convulsing thing in chains stared at Dolan as he stared back smiling ear to ear at it. A gloved latex hand removed the gag that had housed all this evening's screams, opened the mouth, and with the other hand, Dolan inserted the pedophile's cock and balls. He stood there admiring his work and enjoying his craftiness before stating, "You have something in your teeth," and howled laughter, then added, "God forgives. I do not. Go with that."

No more than a matter of seconds passed, and the thing in the chains was gone. Dolan removed the skin that remained, threw it into the washer, and ran a cycle. "These stains will never come out. What have you been into?" he asked the skinned man with a smirk on his face. Next, he put his tools back in their bag, removed his own blood-soaked attire, and deposited them into a plastic bag, then went out the way he'd entered. He'd entered a basement and exited a tomb.

"Memories pressed between the pages of my mind, memories sweetened through the ages just like wine." Behind the wheel of his custom ride, he sang Elvis's song to himself and was all smiles as he drove past the rear entrance of James and Shelia's property. Less than three minutes, he would arrive at the main house. No more time for reminiscing now. Perhaps after everything was put in place for the night's grand finale, there would be time to reflect once again. Relive in his mind the sex trafficker's brutal deaths. How he'd turned them into human shishkabobs for the benefit of James. First things first though. He had to prepare the house and get things set up for James's arrival.

According to the timeline Dolan had established for James to follow, he should be arriving at the Wyoming address any moment. Afterward, he would be on his way to the same location that Dolan was currently entering into the driveway of, thus bringing the game to a close, one way or the other.

As the SUV entered the driveway, excitement anew flowed through him. The anticipation was creeping in as he drove around to the rear of the house, pulled off the driveway and around the back of the garage to dock the land barge out of sight from the road. Dolan shut the engine off, exited the vehicle, and went to the back of the SUV, checking the camera where Shelia was from his phone to make sure she was still out. "Sleeping like a baby," he spoke into the night. Dolan popped the back door, opened the factory hatch, then hit the remote for his custom body compartment and retrieved the body. With the body fetched, all compartments and doors closed, he made his way to back of the house. Motion lights came on, helping him along.

Police had taped off the house but were long gone by now, and they'd felt it unnecessary to leave an officer to keep watch. The house had plenty of security, and Shelia was being watched at the hospital. So they thought. Dolan was aware of all security measures at the house. All he needed was Shelia's thumbprint to open the door and then a quick scan again inside to prevent alarms from sounding. Not only did he have the thumb, but he had the rest of her as well. He smirked.

After he gained entry and scanned the thumb again inside, the system said, "Welcome home, Shelia."

"Thank you. It's good to be back," Dolan answered for her, smirking as he carried her through the kitchen, into the hallway past the living room and around a corner into the grand entryway of the house. Though coming in through the back way, it was still grand indeed. They had spared little, if any, expense on the house.

An immediate left led to the left stairwell, which he ascended, noting the bloodstained floor, walls, ceiling, steps, and handrail on the right staircase that he would soon be cleaning to prepare for James's arrival. It wouldn't do for him to see this mess. That was not part of the game. Besides, Dolan hadn't created this particular scene, so it didn't matter to him if anyone had seen it or not. It was not his artistry.

At the top of the staircase, he made another left down a corridor that opened into the master suite. Dolan entered the room and placed Shelia on the bed. Afterward, he grabbed a clean set of pajamas and changed her out of her hospital garb into something more for the occasion. Once dressed, he lay her in position as if she were sleeping and folded her hands on her chest before injecting her once more with a small dose.

She looked like a body in a casket, exactly like he wanted. Next, he walked over to a table just aside the French doors, removed a piece of stationery and pen, wrote three words on it before taking it to the bedroom door and sticking it to the outside. Finally, with the scene set to his liking, he pulled the door almost tight but not quite, then descended the same flight they'd ascended together.

Again, he looked at the mess at the foot of the stairwell across the room and dreaded the cleaning it would require of him to make things presentable. "Oh well, it must be done," he muttered to himself, "but at least it will give me time to take a walk down memory lane once more." He smirked as he made his way to the closet where the cleaning supplies were kept. Once more, Elvis began to sing "Memories" in his mind as he twirled Shelia's hospital gown in the air, slow dancing up the hall like a deranged Fred Astaire.

Chapter 9

Standing in the basement where James himself had been not long before them, the officers were trying to understand what they were looking at. The sight before them was reminiscent of what Deke and Fore had witnessed at the Seaverses' home earlier that evening. That was when Deputy Fore finally lost what small grip he had been holding on to the situation with altogether. "That's it. I'm finished. I'm out. Finato. I am done. I've seen enough gore in one night to last a lifetime. In fact it's not even been a whole night yet, only a few short hours since we found whatever it was we found at the Seaverses' house. I can't take any more of this. I am gone. Sorry, Sarge. I hate to bail out on you, but even Bon Jovi is starting to sound like a better idea to see than this nightmare anymore. I'm going home. Don't call me. I'll call you, and I wouldn't hold your breath. If they want to fire me, so be it. In fact I may save them the trouble. Best of luck to you all, I hope you catch whoever or whatever you're chasing, but do me a favor and don't fill me in on it. No, thank you." And with that, Deputy Fore was indeed finished for the evening as well as the foreseeable future.

Captain Higgins looked at Sergeant Deke with a raised eyebrow, a wondering look, and asked "Bon Jovi?" With Fore gone, the lieutenant called over Officer Compton, who up to this point had remained silent all night with the exception of some snickering, undoubtedly at the expense of Deke and Fore themselves.

"I guess some people just can't handle the pressure." He addressed Higgins but was talking to Deke. Deke dismissed his comment knowing it was not only a poke at Fore himself but also a dig at their small-town police force. "The smell in here is almost unbearable. Grab the laptop. The sergeant and I will read it outside while you call this in from your car. And remember what I told you when we first got to Slane."

"Yes, sir," Compton answered Higgins.

Compton carefully retrieved the laptop, then followed up the stairs as quickly as his out-of-shape body could muster. The exertion, on top of the smell which had been churning at his previous meal, already was now telling his body it was about to evacuate all the contents of his stomach. Fast as his bulk could move, he ran down the hall toward the front door trying to make it outside before the vomit exploded all over the crime scene. As he exited the house, the contents erupted and filled his mouth. Compton tightened his lips and covered his mouth trying to keep it in until he reached the railing. Once he reached the rail, he hit it so hard he thought he may topple over. That would make the situation even more humiliating.

The railing stood fast though, and he remained right side up, but all the contents that were previously in his gut were now flying out over the railing. Vomit took flight as being launched, went airborne, and hit the windshield of his vehicle, coloring it in chunks of undigested supper. The second wave came quick but with less fury. Unable to make it all the way to the windshield, this time it hit against his driver door window. Rather would have hit the window had he not left it rolled down. Thus, most of the second wave of regurgitation found its way into the interior of his car, decorating his steering wheel, console, inner door, and his seat with the warm bile. The majority of which landed where he had to park his fat rear shortly.

Sgt. Deke, who was standing on the far end of the porch along with Higgins and out of harm's way, smiled and only repeated what Compton had told him mere minutes before. "I guess some people just can't handle the pressure." This actually did bring a small chuckle from Higgins, who then added with great sarcasm, "I hope you threw up all over the laptop, you pile of monkey nuts." Then he walked over to Compton and jerked it away before more puke had a chance to hit it.

"I held it behind me the whole time. There's nothing on it," Compton answered feebly and with embarrassment.

"Let's keep it that way. Pull yourself together and do what I told you to do. Can you handle that or do we need to try to catch Fore and get him back on board? At least he doesn't make messes."

"No, sir, I'm fine now. I'll make that call."

"Good. The adults will be over here reading the email." Higgins turned to join Deke at the far end again. As he walked away, he heard another heave and upchuck as more undigested food exited Compton. Higgins closed his eyes and rolled them in their sockets. "Douche nugget," he said to himself. Then to Deke, "Lets open this over at my car. It's the furthest away from his. Hopefully we don't get hit by anything that far away."

"Let's hope," Sarge agreed as they walked toward his vehicle.

At the car, Higgins laid the laptop on the roof and brought up the screen they needed. Each read in silence, waiting for the other to speak first when finished. Deke was the one who broke the silence. "If anyone sexually abused my daughter, I wouldn't care at all what happened to the person who done it myself. In fact if everything this email says is true, and I have no doubt that it is, I care a whole lot less now than when we started about catching this guy. I don't agree with his methods 100 percent, but I can't argue with the results."

"It's not his job to get justice. That's my job. I mean our job. And we're going to catch this freak. That's exactly what he is. Even if everything is true in the email, it's not his place to do what he's doing. I think he just uses their sins as an excuse to kill because he thinks he's so high and mighty. You can tell the way he writes. He's cocky, arrogant, and thinks he's above the law. I personally take offense to that. After all, I am, rather we, are the law. The system sucks, I know, but we can't have vigilante justice no matter how much you or anyone else may agree with it.

Compton, who had apparently finally finished expelling his stomach's contents, had placed his call and was now reading the email as Deke and Higgins carried on their conversation. "I'm trying to figure out what James has to do with this. Why was he chosen for this "game," as the Writer calls it? The only one playing a game is the man leaving the emails. It's no game to anyone else. In fact I think James may be a victim in this too. I haven't got it all figured out yet, naturally, but some of the pieces are starting to come together. I want to get to Wyoming and read that next email. If we're lucky, maybe we'll be close enough to catch James still there too. But I seriously doubt it."

Compton, who had finished reading the email, added his two cents to the conversation. "He's got a sick sense of humor."

"Really, you think so? Higgins scoffed. "Thanks for that insight, Captain Obvious. Why don't you let the adults have the conversation?"

Probably loves Bon Jovi, Deke thought to himself. Higgins told Compton to get over to Wyoming but wait for them to get there before going in.

"It doesn't make sense," Deke told Higgins. "Why is he involving James in this? I mean, the man in the basement and the man in the chair were both sexually hurting children in one form or another, right? That's why there were tortured and killed. Obviously, James knew nothing about what these men had done or what they were; otherwise, the Writer wouldn't be explaining his reasoning for it all at each new location. Is it sounding to you like maybe James is being punished? Being taught a lesson of some kind? If James was guilty of crimes such as those we've found so far tonight, why wouldn't the Writer just have killed him too already and been done? What's the freaking point? What are we not seeing?"

"As I said, I'm starting to put a theory together here, but I want to see the next email before I share it. Now let's get over there and find the next piece to the puzzle." Higgins shut the laptop, opened his door, and tossed it into the passenger seat before getting in himself. Deke retrieved his own car, and both men pulled out of one grotesque crime scene heading for another, where neither would believe what they had seen.

*****

Just what was the Writer doing at his private address? Was Shelia his final victim? Surely, she had been taken to the hospital for observation, he assured himself, thus out of harm's way. Plus, so far, he hadn't killed anyone except sex offenders, and Shelia certainly didn't fall into that category. James had followed all the rules of the game, done exactly as he had been instructed. He'd attempted to include no one in the game. He made every destination from one grotesque scene to the next in the allotted time. So just what was waiting for him when he got home?

The Writer had promised he'd not hurt her if James played by the rules, but of course, the guy was a raving lunatic. Maybe it had something to do with all the blood he left at his home. He still had no idea where it all came from. Had he killed someone this crazy mad writer knew and was being punished and taunted? Sometimes there were serial killers that worked in pairs. Maybe James thought he killed one of them, and now the other was playing with him.

No, that doesn't make much sense, he told himself. If there had been two killers, surely, the Writer would have mentioned the other in at least one of the emails. It seemed that great pains had been taken to set everything up this evening. It had to have been planned and thought out well with great care. No spur of the moment revenge game to get even. Just questions and more questions James felt like his mind was beginning to unravel.

Finally it hit him. "I'm the end game," he spoke out loud. After all, the entire night had been set up specifically for him. To teach him a lesson, to taunt him, for revenge. Whatever the reason was, he didn't know, but he was sure now that he was the last piece of the madman's so-called art. Positive now that when he got home, he would somehow be murdered and displayed in some kind of sick, twisted display to be found by police.

But I've never had anything to do with any kind of sex offense. I'm nothing like the men I came across tonight. That isn't the point though, is it? No. There is a method to the madness, and though I'm not sure yet what my part is in this, I know he'll indulge me once I arrive.

The first victim had watched child pornography, so his eyes had been taken. The hand removed, probably the one he jerked with as he watched. The second had raped children. His skin had been removed, and he tried to be washed clean of his sins. He had loved fellatio performed on him by children, boys mostly, so the Writer had reversed the concept and inserted the man's own cock into his mouth after being sliced off.

The two human shishkabobs that were sex traffickers had been taken apart and rearranged, signifying the ruining of innocent lives and families they had torn apart and destroyed. Though some could be put back together or heal, they were never the same. He also quite believed the Writer when he wrote that he had churned their insides to butter. James was positive they died horribly, and to be honest, he didn't have much pity for them or for any of the night's victims.

The greater the crime, the worse the punishment. The man in the chair had been lucky he had only watched. The sentencing has been light. *What will my punishment be?* he asked. *I'm nothing like them. What if*—Then he snapped back from his rabbit hole he had been running down. "Okay, okay, stop it. All right, get ahold of yourself. I'm starting to lose it. Not only am I talking to myself now; I'm starting to answer back." He was talking to himself in the SUV. "How long have I been awake?" James wasn't sure.

He remembered nothing leading up to the moment he came to in the master bedroom, standing at the foot of their bed. It was like a memory no longer there. James slapped himself twice, trying to snap out of his frame of mind. *I have to stop thinking about it*, he told himself. James was pulling into the driveway of the guesthouse now. Best not to go to the main house in vehicle. Besides, going on foot could give him an advantage, he thought.

The thought occurred to him that police could still be there waiting for his return. Could that be what the Writer was doing? Bringing him back to the scene of the crime only to be confronted by police? No, that wasn't right either. Somehow James knew he was going to face his adversary in person. That's what the plan had been the whole time. This whole evening was about him and the Writer coming together.

James looked at his watch. Almost six hours had passed since he opened the first email. Now here he was, home again. The evening had brought him full circle. Hitting the garage door opener as the pickup neared the guesthouse, James got a look at himself in the rearview mirror. How tired and haggard he looked. *How much have I aged in the last six hours?* he wondered. *I look ten years older. After everything I've seen tonight and all the worrying, it's no wonder. I'm lucky to still be sane, and that may not last much longer.*

As he parked the truck, James retrieved the 9mm from the console and exited the cab, left the garage through the side door, and pushed the garage door opener on the wall as he went out sealing the truck inside. Immediately heading to the main house, he was hit with a thought—the laptop in the guesthouse. Every stop tonight involved a laptop with a message. Was there, by chance, another one inside waiting for him here? He'd already been here and found a message earlier this evening or late last night, however you want to say it. It was possible though that the Writer had come back again and left a second email. After all, the Writer wasn't stupid. He knew that if James came back to the main house, he would stop here first. So much for the element of surprise. *I better check to make sure,* he thought. Maybe there are final instructions for this repulsive game.

Turning toward the guesthouse, he froze in place. What if someone is dead inside here and displayed for his amusement? His mind raced. Who could it be? Was it a trap? More freaking questions. "I'm sick of questions. Fed up with questions and then some. I just want this to end already." Anger was starting to grow and to push him forward, beginning to leave rationality behind. James took the safety off and entered the guesthouse.

One light was on inside and shone through the darkness of the rooms between it and the front door, just enough to make out almost nothing. It appeared to be coming from the office. He stood where he was, allowing his eyes to adjust to the dark rather than turn on more lights. Vigilantly, he went to the hallway, turned, and made his way toward the office, ready for anything to happen. Reaching the office, he noticed the laptop sitting on the desktop and not as he had left it. The laptop was open, facing him as he entered the room, and no doubt had a message waiting. Like too many times this evening, James opened an email that he didn't want to read or have any part of.

THE WRITER

Fifth email:

> Hello, James. I figured you would stop by here before heading up to the main house. I would have done the same. Plus, I have enough faith in you to believe you also would assume a final message could be waiting for you here before you tarried onward. You're an intelligent man, James. I wonder if you're intelligent enough to have figured out what your role is in all this yet? If not, don't worry. I won't think any less of you. Besides, you've had a busy evening and perhaps have been a little overwhelmed. I will explain everything once you arrive, and finally, all of your questions will be answered.
>
> So have you learned anything tonight, James? I hope so. I'd hate for this whole game to have been played for nothing. Sure, I had a blast setting it all up and creating the masterpieces you seen this evening, but it's also meant for you to learn as well. I do hope you have learned something, James. Why don't you head on up and we'll discuss everything. There's just one more thing before you go that I need you to do for me.
>
> Return the gun to the safe. Under no circumstances are you to bring it with you. That would be bad for Shelia, and I know you don't want that. You may decide to shoot first and ask questions later. That would be no fun. I promise I don't have one either. I never use guns. They create more problems than they solve.
>
> Your laptop has a camera built in, and I'm watching you as I have done from every laptop at every stop you made tonight. So all you need do is turn the laptop 180 degrees and let me see you put the 9mm back in its place.

James turned the laptop and walked over to the safe, making sure the view was clear, and housed the 9mm back to its place, his anger growing larger.

> Thank you, James. I knew I could count on you to follow the rules, but to be safe, keep the laptop open and focused on the safe when you leave. Just in case you would double back. I've removed the police tape around the house for you so it feels more like coming home rather than to a crime scene. I also took care of a small problem with a little piggy named Jasper who was at your guesthouse when I returned. He would only have complicated things for us. You can thank me later. I even cleaned up the mess you made in the entryway. You really went to town on someone, didn't you? Blood was everywhere. It looked like a mess I could have made. Lol.
>
> Now, James, the moment you've been waiting for is at hand. The reason why all of this was done, the reason why you have played this game for so long is finally here. The time has come for us to meet face-to-face. Time to get all the answers you desire. So come, James, come and let us finish our beautiful game… Come.

Saying nothing or giving any hint of the anger swelling inside him, James turned and walked out of the office, up the hall, through the kitchen, and vacated the house. Once outside, he pulled the door and stood there looking into the woods that lay between him and the main house, and pondered.

It sounds like he has Shelia there, but how? Surely, she'd been taken to the hospital. Maybe she had been released already? Maybe she hadn't needed to go? Unlikely, but it was a possibility. Unless… his mind wondered. *No, that's impossible. Could the Writer have got her from the hospital, somehow? No, that's crazy, James.* Still, somehow, he knew she was up there with him. Was his intention to serve them up as a duo display like the two men that had been rearranged? More, the anger grew.

Standing there staring into the darkness, James began to smile a cold dark smile. One that came with the unhinging of reality. As he started toward the garage, the smile widened. James entered the garage, went to the back of the truck, and lowered the tailgate. Inside was the instrument that had been waiting there for him all night. Whispering to him at every stop, every short drive between displays, like a small whisper in the back of his brain growing louder and louder but going unheard, until now.

Of course, the Writer would see it easily. It couldn't be concealed. But it would come with him regardless. Reaching into the truck bed, he grabbed what had been laying there in wait for his return and calling out to him since the game began. The very thing that had been dripping blood all over his house mere hours ago. It was time to make it sing once more. Holding it up to the moonlit sky, he glared at the head as it reflected only small glimmers of metal due to the fact it was covered almost entirely in coagulated blood, and beheld…his axe.

Chapter 10

"For the first time in all my years on the force, I'm speechless. I have no idea what to say. I'm not even sure I know what I'm looking at."

"What are you talking about?" Higgins asked Deke. "The bodies are over here."

"Yeah, I'm quite aware of where the bodies are. By this time, I gotta say I don't find them all that disturbing, and to be honest, I'm sure whatever they did to deserve this was even worse than what happened to them. Every scene we've been to tonight, the crimes committed get greater and so does the punishment. But I'm not sure anyone deserves to have to see this." Sgt. Deke was looking at the mural of the two men painted on the opposite side of the room from where the men on the couch were positioned. "This is the most god-awful thing I've seen tonight. How in the name of all that is holy could someone purposely have this on their wall? If they weren't dead already, I'd kill them myself. I mean I don't know a lot about art. In fact, what I don't know could fill a book, but this is hideous. I think the Writer may actually be doing the world a favor. Not only for eliminating sex offenders but by abolishing anyone with the opinion that this was a good idea or good art as well. Look at this piece of—"

That's when he noticed the vinyl record collection and record player in the corner. The cover in the front of the stack was Bon Jovi—Slippery When Wet. "It's official, these two deserved to die."

"Okay," Higgins told him, "I get it. The painting sucks. The pile of cocaine we seen on the way in would explain a lot of it. I think you've rambled long enough. Can we get back to what matters and leave the art for the critics?"

"I wouldn't ever call it art, but yeah, I think I've deflected long enough. Like I said though, whatever these two did, I'm sure the

THE WRITER

punishment was deserved. You and I may not agree with it, but I guarantee you that whatever they did is something bad enough that I won't feel sorry for them."

Higgins and Deke went to the laptop and read the message. Deke broke the silence first. "I told you that painting sucked. Even a raving psycho knows it's horrible. And he's crazy."

"Enough with the painting, okay. Will you focus? I want to catch this sicko. As long as he isn't lying, there's one stop left. Right back to where this all began. James has to be on his way there now or is already there. Doing the math from the time you all arrived at the Seaverses' and the first body we found, we shouldn't be far behind him."

"I'll call headquarters. They can send someone now."

"No," Higgins shouted. You'll do no such thing. You were told by your commander to follow my lead, and that's what I expect you to do. If you call now, they'll beat us by a long shot and someone else will get the credit. Is that what you really want? Be honest? We've been chasing this Loony Tune all night. Tracking through blood, breathing in stench, digesting gore, being forced to look at his insane art, reading his smug emails, your own deputy even quit on you. Do you really want someone else to grab him after all that? After all we've had to go through. Or do you want to slap the cuffs on this murderer, which is what he really is no matter how you look at it, as badly as I do?"

Deke said nothing. Only stood there thinking about everything Higgins had just said and recalling the evening's events. The Seaverses' house seemed like such a long time ago, and now he was heading back there again, it appeared.

Yes! He did want to catch the mad artist. Not for glory. Not for justice. Not because he was close to retiring and this would be a fantastic ending to a solid but not glorious career. Not to show up Deputy Fore who had ran out on him or anyone else on the force either. No not for any of those reasons. Just one reason and one reason only. He wanted to catch him, pure and simple. He'd been chasing him all night, and he was so close now. He could taste it.

"One condition," Deke proclaimed. "When we get close enough to beat everyone there, I call it in and I get to put the cuffs on. You can take all the glory and credit, I don't care, but I get to cuff him."

"Sounds good to me. Let's go. I'll be right behind you."

As they exited the room, Sarge took one last look at the travesty painted on the wall and thought to himself shaking his head, *I'm still not sure what was the greater crime in there.*

*****

Dolan sat in a corona bench with blue suede cushions that sat in the hallway just outside James and Shelia's master bedroom. The bench was for decoration, not for use, which Shelia would have informed him of if she were not unconscious on the other side of the bedroom door. From his position, he could see through the railing spindles with a complete view of the front door and foyer. If James decided to come through the rear or side entrance, he still had to enter the second floor by the staircase, and Dolan had full view of either side.

As he sat awaiting the arrival of his guest, Dolan began to reminisce once more of events that had unfolded leading to this evening's main event. All the sweet suffering that had transpired. As he focused his gaze on the foyer below his throne of suede, he relived the abduction of the two sex traffickers. They had been the greatest work of his game, though not his most favorite to create. That honor belonged to the man in the basement. Oh, how sweet it had been. *I wish it could have lasted longer*, he thought. The two traffickers had been a lot of fun as well, but everyone has their druthers.

The man in the chair and the man in the basement had been easy pickings. Each lived alone and neither had an alarm system or a dog. The coke brothers, however, lived together, had a security system, and a dog as well. The security system was nothing Dolan hadn't bypassed before in previous games, and the dog would be easy to dispose of. He'd killed almost as many dogs as humans; he hated dogs. Ever since he'd been bitten as a child, he couldn't stand the foul beasts. Sometimes he killed them just because. But those were thoughts for another day.

The trick would be capturing the prey without confrontation. Not because he was afraid of confrontation or didn't like it.

THE WRITER

Sometimes he welcomed it. However, these two had a specific purpose to serve, and he didn't want them bruised, tarnished, scraped, scratched, or harmed in any way before their time. Like a painter who wants a clean blank slate to begin their work, so did this artist. He liked his canvases to be as pristine as possible when he started carrying out his sentencing.

He wanted to administer all the punishment he so desired to a blank canvas. Not one that had already been beaten, stabbed, or shot. That's why he used needles. Needles made with his personal homemade concoction. Once they were subdued carefully and on his table, then the brutality could come.

The traffickers lived in a cul-de-sac, and the house next to theirs was being renovated. As mentioned before, when it came to killing, Dolan was exceptional at it and also had a tendency to get lucky, a lot. He had been watching their house from the lot next door after contractors were finished for the day, getting an idea of when would be the right time to intervene.

Finally, after several days of close observation, the night had arrived. Dolan had been watching from next door, making sure no one was left inside before making his way over. After quickly bypassing the alarm, he went to the back door knowing the hellhound waited inside. Once he opened the door, he had no doubt it would be lying in wait. He would use no weapon or special needle; instead, he would take great pleasure in killing the beast with his bare hands.

Standing outside the door, Dolan listened. Not a sound came from inside, but he knew the fowl creature was in wait. Finally he picked the lock and slowly pushed the door open. Inch by inch, it crept until the door was opened as wide as it could go. Nothing waited immediately inside the doorway. Dolan stared into an empty kitchen. "I know you're here, you little bastard." Still nothing. Without turning around, Dolan pulled the door close and inched forward, expecting an attack at any moment.

"I know you're in here, you filthy mongrel. Show yourself." Still, only silence. As he began to make his way out of the kitchen into the hall, he heard a low growl. The sun, not entirely down yet, lit a small light through the hall and reached into small dark recesses of the rooms, but not enough to see where the dog was hiding. Dolan stood in place. "I can't see you but I can smell you, you nasty ball licker. I'm going to break your neck and dislocate your jaw for you. Won't that be nice?"

Dolan didn't want to turn on any lights. He wasn't sure how long it could be before one or both arrived home, and he dared not tip his hand to them showing up and noticing lights on that should be off. Instead, he inched forward in the dark. Finally, as he cleared the doorway, the last of the evening light showed a sparkle in the room to his right. A quick look and he saw it was the dog's collar reflecting from the failing light. Dolan turned and faced the hound. As he turned toward the house's last line of defense, the Rottweiler bared its teeth and raced toward him. Dolan only smiled.

Standing his ground as the Rott charged, Dolan kept calm. As the dog leaped up to attack, Dolan turned sideways grabbing the dog in midflight around the neck. The force was strong enough to knock him to the ground, but he kept his grip. They hit the ground with Dolan landing atop. Two of the dog's ribs broke from the weight that landed on him. Still, the dog tried to kick, scratch, and bite, and do what he had been trained to do but the position he was in, it was to no avail.

Dolan looked down at the mutt and smiled. "I told you I was going break your neck, didn't I, you little turd wrangler." With one hand wrapped around its neck and his weight holding him to the ground, Dolan took his free hand and began to twist the helpless dog's head around, intending to fulfill his promise. In doing so, the dog began to cry in agony. Then Dolan stopped what he was doing. Never before had he stopped what he was doing because of human cries and certainly not for a dog, but something made him cease the activity he was indulging in.

Something about the way this particular dog had acted in its defense of his domain. It hadn't attacked with all-out abandon. It didn't just bark and try to scare him away. It had laid in wait, luring him in, almost playing with him. This dog reminded him of himself. For the first time in his life, or at least since he'd been bitten in youth, Dolan felt like for a dog. *Maybe I'm just crazy*, he mused, *but I think he may be worth letting live.*

THE WRITER

Still not willing to chance an attack, Dolan pulled out a syringe and sent the four-legged assassin to la-la land rather than to the hereafter. *If I'm wrong, I can dispose of him later, but until that time maybe I'll see how it feels to be a dog owner.* After the needle did its job, he returned the partial syringe to his case and carried his new pet over to the couch and gently lay him down. "It's not your fault your owners are vile pieces of human dung and are going to die. I'll bandage those ribs for you later. For now, sleep."

After his new friend was made comfortable as could be under the circumstances, Dolan went to the front door and began his watch through the darkened glass that lined each side of the entry door. Easy to see out, nearly impossible to see in, and he waited for the first arrival of the evening.

After watching and waiting almost thirty minutes, a car pulled into the driveway. Two men got out and approached the door, neither of whom lived here. Dolan peered through the peephole as they approached. A loud obnoxious knock came at the door. He heard the two men talking outside as they waited for an answer. The conversation was about the blow they were there to purchase and some new female company for the evening's festivities. Each were laughing and already sniffing, showing signs that coke was already fueling future events.

Looks like a change in plans, Dolan thought. It appears we'll be having four tonight. Not a problem. However, if this was going to be a coke party, there could be more than he could deal with in one evening. If it was just these two and the ones he waited for, he could handle it, no problem. Cokeheads were capable of anything, the least of which is any kind of common sense or rationality.

His mind shifted gears, and almost without trying, a new plan was hatched. Dolan spoke through the door to the would-be rapist, "Go around back. It's open." Dolan quickly moved to the back door, which he had locked after drugging the dog, to unlock it once more. After doing so, he left the kitchen and stepped inside the bathroom that was on the left wall heading into the living room. Inside, he pulled the door only enough so he could watch them pass through the crack between the door and the jam.

The back door opened, and laughter spilled into the room, followed by two cokeheads yapping a mile a minute and being so loud that they would never hear him coming. If the door he was behind squeaked when he opened it, they would never know. In fact, they were so high he wasn't sure they would even know what hit them. Deciding not to waste a lot of precious time on them, inflicting pain they would not feel anyway, he decided to end them quickly. Besides, they were not part of his plan. Under other circumstances, he would attack and wait for the effects of the coke to wear off to inflict punishment, but tonight he couldn't do that, unfortunately. One of the men who was a participant in his plans could arrive at any moment, so he had to work fast.

Upon entering, they closed the door behind them and yelled out the names of the ones they sought. "Yo! Where you at?" followed by the second proclaiming, "We came for our bitches and blow," which made both men laugh. "We're horny and running low on the snow."

Again, the first one spoke, "Let's see what the snowman has. We brought plenty of Benjamins. The last sentence was spoken as they passed the bathroom doorway en route to the billiard room.

Dolan swung the door open and stepped out into the hall, walking behind them, be they oblivious to the fact. As they turned and entered into the billiard room, Dolan closed the distance. Just inside the entry, they looked around and had seen no one inside. What they did see, however, was almost a kilo of cocaine in a brick sitting out on the table.

"Well look what we have here. Whoo! It's gonna be that kind of night. Let's get it started already. Where you at?" This was from the second man.

"I'm sorry. I'm afraid the men you're looking for aren't here at the moment, but I expect them back very soon, so we have to make this quick. The two newcomers turned to see who was addressing them. When they saw the masked man who greeted them was not their supplier, they were thrown off. Each man looked dumbfounded. They couldn't decide if they were being messed with or if this was a real situation. They looked at each other, then back at the man they were in question of.

THE WRITER

Dolan stepped forward. They recoiled. "Hey, bro, stop this. It ain't funny all right."

"I know it's not funny. In fact it's quite the opposite. You two showed up at the wrong time. Well, the wrong time for you but at the perfect time for me. As I said, this has to be quick, so if you don't mind, I must dispense with the pleasantries." Dolan pulled out a switchblade and pushed the button, dispensing an eight-inch blade. No needles for these two. Just a quick death which they didn't deserve, but time was of the essence.

Again, he approached. This time, one of the men reached behind their back reaching for his pistol. Dolan raced forward with uncanny speed, and before the weapon could be drawn, he drove the knife up under the chin, through the teeth over the gums. *Watch out brain. Here it comes*, he thought to himself. The knife sunk all the way in until the handle stopped it from going further.

Still clutching the knife, the second unexpected visitor had picked up a pool cue, turned, and was swinging it at him. Ducking before the blow could land and pulling the blade free from the other man at the same time, allowing him to fall to the ground, dead before he hit the floor, Dolan used his free hand to snag the pool cue assailant around the neck after his swing missed target and drew him near. In a secure death grip headlock, he took the blade and drove it through the right temple, through the skull, into the brain, and out the other side. Only a few small kicks and spasms, and the man was gone. Letting him fall to the floor, he looked them over, then bent down and used the last victim's shirt sleeve to clean the blood from his blade before closing it and returning it to his pocket.

With a quickness of stealth rather than one of panic, Dolan pulled the bodies into the nearest closet. The same one he was planning on inhabiting himself as his first trophy returned home. Once inside, he fetched the keys from the driver's pockets and went outside, giving a look up the dead-end road for approaching traffic, seeing nothing coming, and went to the house that served as his lookout for the last week to open the garage door.

The door opened, and Dolan exited. Again, he checked the road for an approaching vehicle before making a quick trot to the

Challenger. Inside, he started the sports car and pulled it out of the space it occupied and into the garage next door. Once the car was out of sight, he stepped out, walked to the wall button, and lowered the garage door. *Nice wheels*, he told himself, then returned to the house next door to stand watch for his desired occupants. After returning to the lookout post, he didn't have to wait more than fifteen minutes before one of the men he waited for returned.

As Dolan stood monitoring through the front door peephole, one of the traffickers returned and headed toward the house. As he approached, Dolan slid into the closet just inside the entry door to wait for the appropriate time to triumph. Behind the closet door, Dolan heard the dead bolt turn and listened as the waste of life entered. He heard the door close, followed by the sound of footsteps walking up the hall.

Dolan opened the door slowly, without sound, as the prey walked by. With a quickness few could imitate, he left the closet and snatched the man around the neck with his left hand. Already holding the syringe in his right, he plunged it into his neck and distributed the venom. Within seconds, he was out like a light. Dolan threw him over his shoulder like a sack of potatoes and carried him up to his room where he zip-tied his hands and feet together and ball-gagged his mouth.

There really was no need for any of it. The dose he had given the pervert would knock him out for hours, but Dolan thought it was fun. After he finished, he went back to his post to watch for the second trophy of the night. Again, he stood vigilant, piercing through the door's lens. The sun completely gone now, the security lights shone bright enough to illuminate the surroundings, necessary enough for him to see all that was needed.

Without panic or distress, he continued to watch for a solid hour. Finally, around three o'clock, a vehicle approached; the man he had waited for had arrived. "Finally, we can get down to business," he spoke to his new pet that was still knocked out on the couch. As he watched, the man went around to the passenger side of the vehicle, opened the door, and pulled out two females—two females who looked awfully young.

THE WRITER

It was obvious they were not willing participants of what lay in store. After both girls were out of the vehicle, the trafficker followed close behind, so close he was pressed against them as to keep them from fleeing. This time, Dolan didn't use the closet. Instead, he walked into the first room to the right to await their arrival.

The lock turned, and the trio entered. The trafficker was screaming obscenities but was so wasted he was incoherent. One thing that was understandable was the cries and sobbing of the unwilling escorts. Dolan heard the door shut, and then the sound of a backhand smacking one of the girls. Another cry rang out, then more laughter before another slap. Dolan waited and listened.

The room from which he watched and listened had no door, only an opening that was almost nine feet wide. He heard more sobbing, then one of the girls went flying by the room entry headfirst and hit hard before she slid another three feet. As she regained some control, she rolled over, sitting on the floor, and began to push herself away from the belligerent assailant. Next came a sound of leather hitting flesh. Dolan knew that sound all too well. Then another loud cry. The second girl had entered the view, and as she did, he noticed the belt again, ringing true to its course. The girl was hit in the face, and almost immediately, a purple bulb began to rise. Next, she too went sprawling forward, landing atop the other girl.

By this time, Dolan's blood was so hot he wasn't sure if he could restrain himself. He wanted to kill this guy here and now, but he knew he had to keep his cool and follow the procedure that was intended for the game. He must follow the plan.

The fourth victim of the night finally entered into view, with his arm raised, ready to deliver another blow to whoever was in its path. He didn't care who it hit; he just wanted to invoke fear and harm. The girls, both on their rears now, sliding away from the leather strap and he who whaled it, were crying uncontrollably. The heathen drew closer to the girls, raining blows of leather. Some hitting their target, some not.

The girls backed up now as far as they could go, held each other tightly, crying and wishing they were anywhere else in the world as another lash found its mark. Dolan had had enough. Moving out of the shadows that hid him, Dolan reached the man as he was coming forward with another swat of leather. As the man's arm came forward Dolan grabbed it, sending a sharp pain up the belted arm. Even through the drunken fog, the pain struck home. Something had torn in his shoulder, a rotator cuff perhaps. With more force than he wanted to administer but was now temporarily able to control, Dolan twisted the hand with the belt with such force in the wrong direction the wrist snapped. The cry that came was unsatisfactory. He wanted to hear more.

Still holding the broken wrist, he shifted his weight, forcing the man to his knees holding the arm straight out behind him. With his free arm and upper body weight Dolan smashed into the back of his elbow, shattering the joint and making his arm bend the opposite direction. The cries of agony that filled the room were like sweet music.

The two girls, already beside themselves, now fell even deeper into incoherence. As their cries began to somber out of shock, the man's began to rise. Not wanting to hurt his art beforehand, he was now helpless to resist. The anger, almost impossible to hold back, was coming forth. Besides, what could it hurt to let go a little in this case? What lay in store for him was total rearrangement of body parts anyway. Did it really matter if he started a little early this time?

The man with the broken elbow turned from his crouched position to see who had intervened with his plans. In doing so, he was greeted with a leather fisted glove that smashed his nose breaking it and sending fresh blood from the nostrils. Letting go of the arm, Dolan kicked the man in the seat of his pants with a force that sent him flying forward and landing hard.

His right arm useless, nose broke, blood flowing, the wounded man crawled toward the two girls begging for help as they cowered against the wall. *You got to be kidding me*, Dolan thought. What nerve he had. Just as the man reached out, about to grab one of the girls, he was pulled backward, back up the hallway. As he was pulled, the man's nails left scratches in the hardwood floor, while he begged the girls to help him. Once they were clear of the girls, Dolan twisted the foot so hard it turned almost completely around. A scream rang

THE WRITER

through the house, filling Dolan's ears like a symphony of pain. Dolan lifted his head, took in a deep breath, smelled the sorrow, held it, then exhaled.

That was as far as he would allow his unhinging to go tonight. Already he'd allowed it to go further than he wanted. His preference for a blank slate already compromised, he'd let it go no further. At the far end of the hall from where the ladies sat, Dolan took out a needle and used it to shut up the trafficker's cries until he got him back to the torture room where the real cries would begin.

Just before the man was out for the count, Dolan whispered to him, "You will pray for death before I finish what I have in store for you. The pain you feel now will seem like ecstasy in comparison. Now sleep. You need your rest," followed by laughter.

Dolan peered at the two teenage girls curled up together at the far end of the hall, raised his hand to his mouth, raising only his pointer finger, pressing it against his lips, and gave the universal sign to be quiet. "Shh." The girls sat gazing in fear at what they had just witnessed and what may possibly wait in their futures. Dolan wanted to ease their minds quickly to assure them he meant no harm. Raising his arms over his head like a criminal in an old Western movie that had just been apprehended by the good guy, he told them he was only here for the man who was broken and bleeding on the floor.

He began to approach the two, but in doing so, their cries rang out and fresh fear filled their faces. Stopping and standing in place, Dolan reached into his back pocket and brought out a wallet with a fake ID and about $5,000 in cash. One never knew when cash would be necessary. Sometimes cash spoke louder than violence and was quicker to get what was needed.

Opening the wallet, he counted out loud so the girls could hear until he got to $2000. Replacing the wallet, Dolan walked over to the table inside the doorway and placed the wad of cash next to the lamp. Not sure if either girl was old enough to drive, he retrieved the keys from the man's pocket anyway and placed them on the cash. Looking at the wounded youths, he stepped out from between them and the table, walking backward into the room he had been lurking in mere minutes earlier.

Once he was inside the room, he spoke to them. "Go home." Frozen in place, they didn't move. *A trick*, they wondered. *As soon as we grab the cash, he'll grab us.* They spoke nothing. Dolan read it all in their eyes. Leaving the room where he was, Dolan walked to the front door, opened it, and let it stand open before returning to his position. Again, he spoke. "Take the money, the keys, and go home. You are not a part of what comes next. Now go."

Slowly, as understanding began to transpire, the girls rose to their feet. Still clutching one another, they inched up the hallway together, pressed against the wall as they went, not once letting their eyes leave Dolan's. Inch by inch, they crept until they reached the table. Dolan was standing, watching the entire time, hands held high. The girl closest the table reached for the keys and cash, her eyes still focused on Dolan. After she put the cash in her purse, she handed the keys to the older of the two and backed slowly out the door.

Dolan, not wanting to spook them, slowly emerged from the billiard room and softly said, "Close the door and tell anyone you like exactly what happened here tonight." The girl with the car keys reached out, pulled the door close, then both ran to the vehicle and sped away.

Dolan lowered his hands and sighed. *Hero and a new pet owner both in the same night. I never would have guessed that. I guess I must be getting soft?* he mused. Then he looked at the sad sack of failure gimped up on the floor and thought about all the hurt that was waiting for him at the kill site, and a smile lit his face. *No, not me. Never.* Then he withdrew two zip ties and bound the man.

Out at his borrowed van, Dolan retrieved two giant duffel bags that were used in construction to haul debris away in and took them back inside, went upstairs, placed the comatose man in one of the bags and carried him out to the van. Likewise, he reentered the house, placed the second man in the bag, and carried him to the van. After both men were loaded up, he fetched the dog and placed him up front between the bucket seats.

After they were loaded, Dolan pulled the van out of the driveway over to the curb, killed the engine, and walked back to the house being renovated. Once more, he opened the garage door, pulled out

THE WRITER

the Challenger, and backed it into the driveway of the house where he had committed the evening's violence. After he parked, he went inside and removed the dead rapists from the closet, carried them one at a time to the trunk, and closed them inside. Afterward, he pulled the car across the street and parked it on the curbside.

Now back inside the vehicle of the damned, he asked, "Is everyone nice and comfy? Don't worry, it's just a short ride. We'll be there in two shakes. I'm afraid, however, once we arrive you won't be too happy with the accommodations. For great fear, torture, agony, and sorrow await. For you, I mean. For me, it will be a sweet savor to the senses and pure delight." The excitement now was intoxicating. "I have so much planned. I hope you're as anxious as me." He smirked.

With that, he turned the engine, and the motor hummed. They had only regular radio, no serius xm radio, which was lame, but what could you do? It did have a CD player, however. Dolan hadn't tried it until now. After all, he'd only borrowed it a few hours ago. "Wonder what's in here? he asked his sleeping victims. The CD button was pushed, and after a few seconds, the song began to pick up where the owner had shut it off. Bon Jovi was singing about a bed of roses. "I hate you, Jovi." Dolan winced in disgust and ejected the CD.

As he drove, he stared at the CD player, taunting it, "One of these days, Jon, one of these days." As one hand steered the van, the other bent the CD over on itself, snapping it in half before tossing it out the window. Afterward, Dolan wiped his hand on his pants to remove the film of suck that was distributed by the CD.

Together, his new canvases, along with his new pet, drove to the desired location previously selected for the night's main event. There, the real fun would begin, as well the great suffering. Dolan was ready to create a masterpiece.

*****

James left the garage and entered the trail which led to the main house. As he entered the woods, his thoughts were becoming less lucid. His thoughts were becoming solely focused on killing the Writer and ending this mayhem. They should have been concentrated more on saving Shelia and less on killing the Writer, but he couldn't help it. Sure, he wanted to save her, but that was placing second to killing this madman. The anger was now becoming hate, and he could focus only on retaliation from everything he'd been through tonight.

This psycho is going to pay. Pay for everything, or I'm going to die trying, he told himself.

Not a violent man by nature, in fact quite the opposite, James considered himself a good Christian man who was easygoing and levelheaded, but now all he could focus on was killing this sick, twisted man who had entered and defiled his life. Never before had he felt anything close to what was now running him.

The Writer had taunted him all night, from the very first email. A smug, cocky arrogance had gleamed at every email, and now the lunatic was taunting James from his very own house. A house he had designed and built himself. From picking out the very location all the way to the style of faucets, he had created it all from nothing. To be fair, he had not done it all on his own accord. Certainly, Shelia and Chae had helped with many details and had input, but he had made it all happen.

Now he was almost being dared to return to what he had created. This ignited more hatred and rage. Without noticing he was doing so, he began to jog, anger growing greater the closer he came to home. "Come, James," the email had taunted. "Yeah, I'll come," he spoke to the night. "I'll come all right. I'll come and bring an end to this insanity with me." The grip on his axe tightened, his stride quickened, his anger grew, and his grin widened. "Yeah, I'm coming."

Chapter 11

Dolan walked the perimeter of the property one final time before entering the building he'd chosen for the evening's festivities, locked the doors, and set his makeshift alarms should anyone try to enter. The house was far from being complete, and at this hour, it was not likely that anyone would be coming around to work or for anything else. As he descended the stairs into the basement, the first man he'd dosed earlier that evening began to stir.

Both men had been stripped naked and strapped to opposite tables that aligned each other. "Well, well, well, look who finally decided to join us. I was hoping you'd wake soon. I have so much planned for us. You're going to just love it. I'm afraid your partner isn't awake yet, but that's okay. He'll join us shortly. We do have a long night ahead of us though, so we should go ahead and get started."

Dolan raised his evening's first weapon of choice to allow his patient to get a good look at what was coming. He tried to scream and free himself, as so many before had tried to do and also failed in his games. There would be no escape now. Not until death came, and Dolan would make sure that was dragged out as long as time would allow. Both men were in for a reality that they couldn't even fathom.

It was almost two hours before the second man finally opened his eyes, reeling in pain from the beating he'd received earlier that night, and tried to figure out where he was and why he couldn't move. "Look who finally decided to join the party. I bet you're in a world of pain, aren't you? Enjoy and appreciate it because it's the best you're going to feel for the rest of your life. From here on out, it's only going to get worse. Just ask your partner here how much fun he's having."

Dolan had secured the men's heads with a strap across the forehead which held them down but was loose enough that either man could turn their head side to side. As he turned to face the patient on the other table that Dolan had already started on, he tried to shout, but the gag held his screams from exiting. Urine released from his bladder and flowed to the foot of the table and fell into a large pan underneath. Unbeknownst to both men, they were on makeshift autopsy tables. The process planned for each man would be slow and bloody, thus each table had been elevated just enough to allow any and all fluids to drain.

The first victim was mostly red from head to toe. One arm was gone, and a saw blade was sticking in the leg only sawed halfway through. Weak but still alive, he turned to face the man who had just awoke into a hell he couldn't imagine was possible. The look on his face told him more than did the amputated arm or saw either one could. "Make yourself comfortable. We have a long night ahead of us. And one of us is going to enjoy it a whole lot more than the other. Your buddy here is doing much better than I gave him credit for. I thought you were both just useless bile only capable of hurting children, fueled by fake courage from your cocaine. But he is more resilient than anticipated. I'm surprised, and I got to admit, that doesn't happen often. I wonder if you'll surprise me as well."

Turning his head back facing front, he saw Dolan standing over him with a wide grin. One like a happy kid at Christmas who had gotten the very toy he'd wanted. "We're going to find out together. Won't that be fun?" Dolan's homemade tables were made to allow them to be raised or lowered very easily. Thus, the victims could be put in a standing position or lowered, either one in compliance with whatever punishment was being administered at that particular time.

Both had been lying almost horizontally, allowing only a small enough tilt so the fluids could flow away, but now he rose the second man's bed so he had full view of what Dolan was doing to his buddy. "Perhaps you'd like to watch and see what lay in store for you? This time, feces left his body. And fell into the pan beneath.

"I hate when this happens. Now the whole room is going to reek for the next fifteen minutes. That will cost you extra." He smirked

THE WRITER

at the helpless man before returning his attention back to the other, whistling the song "Patience" by Guns N' Roses as he went to work. Grabbing the handsaw, he once more began the slow agonizing process of amputating the first leg—agonizing to the leg's owner, of course; not for Dolan, who was enjoying himself immensely.

As the saw went back and forth, the second patient could hear the bone being chewed away by the blade and the groans of agony from the man who was being sawed away at but could do nothing. "Are you sorry yet or should I keep going?" No answer. One couldn't answer through a ball gag and strapped to a bed. "Still not talking, are we? I guess you want me to continue."

Dolan raised his head from his work without stopping to look at the other victim and see if he was watching or if he had closed his eyes. The man's eyes were closed, not wanting to watch the horror before him. Dolan smirked, lowered his head, and continued to saw and whistle.

After all the man's limbs had been removed, not to mention a few strategic cuts with multiple blades here and there just for excitement, little life was left in the man. "It appears our time together is almost over, I'm afraid, but there is one last thing left before you go. Retrieving the first of the two pool cues he would administer this night, he returned to the table. "I'm going to do to you what you have done to so many innocent young girls. Only I'm going to use this. Do you know what a lobotomy is? Essentially, a needle is driven through the skull into the brain where it is used to sever connections to the prefrontal lobe like a windshield wiper. Wiping away not only madness but reality as well. It was a very crude and useless procedure, also quite barbaric, even by my standards." He laughed.

That's sort of what we're going to do here, only I'm going in the other end, and not only back and forth but in and out as well. During the procedure, just think about all females you raped and allowed others to rape with you, as well those you sold to be raped. Did you show any mercy to them? I venture not. This will conclude our time together, but as for you,"—Dolan turned and spoke to the second rapist—"our fun's just about to get started. Then again to the first man, "You have a few minutes left before you join the hereafter. I suggest you use it in prayer. God will forgive even someone as pathetic as you."

Dolan once more faced the second man and said, "Don't worry, I won't use the same cue on you. That would be unsanitary." His head tilted back with laughter. Then spoke the last words the man with no limbs would ever hear, "Eight ball, corner pocket," before driving the cue as far inside as it would go.

After he expired, Dolan withdrew the cue, placed it against the wall, grabbed the saw once more, and removed his head. As he began to reassemble the body parts to his liking, he heard a whine, a faint whimper that was not from the next patient. The dog he had spared was beginning to wake up. Dolan had created a makeshift bed for the dog with the bags he used to carry his prey. Not planning to take care of dog tonight, or any other for that matter, he lacked the proper medicines. He would do that first thing in the morning. For now, all he could do was give it another dose of doggy chow in a needle to keep it knocked out.

Now he went to the second man who was waiting his turn. "I'm afraid your friend took longer to create than I had anticipated, so you and I may not get to spend as much time together as I'd like, but rest assured it will be quality time." A smile showed his pearly-white teeth. Looking at his watch, he said "I think we still have four good hours left. Besides, it's Saturday night, and no one comes here on Sundays to work. Don't worry, I'll show you everything that you missed when I started on your friend while you were still out. I'm going to basically perform the same procedure on you as well. I might switch it up a little here or there to avoid complacency, but it will end with the same result."

Dolan looked at the man and winked before he lowered the table and repeated the second operation of the night, whistling.

*****

James came out of the woods and into the clearing of his backyard. All lights inside appeared to be off from this point of view. No police vehicles either, only a black SUV that must belong to the

Writer. The brisk jog through the woods had not depleted his anger any. In fact, he was growing angrier the closer he got. James walked slowly now, catching his breath, not wanting to be winded for what certainly would occur upon arriving.

The moon gave enough light to clearly see the yard and surroundings, but James knew the Writer would not be lurking outside. He was in his house waiting on him, daring him, taunting. Still, James stayed alert as he walked the backyard, followed around the side of the house, and up to the front porch. The porch lights were on as though the man inside was expecting company. This ignited more anger.

Heart pounding, he started ascending the stairs to the huge front porch that ran across the larger part of the house. As he approached the front door, he said a final prayer, reached for the handle, and pushed it open. The alarm had been turned off as he knew it would be, and no light shone downstairs. The only light was that from the front porch reaching inside only a few feet before fading into darkness. From inside, his silhouette traced a black shadow in the doorway as the porch light shone behind him. The axe held firm. James stepped inside.

Chapter 12

The Showdown

Dolan had been in deep thought of his two trophies' mutilations from his perch when he was brought back to the present as the door below opened, allowing in fresh light. Dolan sat watching to see what James would do. As he entered the still, dark house, he was greeted with a sense of déjà vu. Not from entering, as he had thousands of times over the years, but something else—a strange kind of familiarity.

Upon entering, James turned the light switch on, not sure it would give its light or not, and was a little surprised when the fixtures lit overhead, illuminating the whole entryway. Stepping further inside, James surveyed his surroundings, a quick glance around the room, before he started toward the staircase. He had to check the bedroom. She was there somehow, he knew it. Just like so many things tonight he just knew, without question.

As he headed toward the staircase, Dolan stood, walked to the banister, which made a wide sweep outward in the middle, almost five feet long and three feet wide, and looked down on James. James, seeing the movement, froze in place, looking up at the man who had caused him so much torment. *Nice touch*, he thought. *I'm sure the fact that he's up there looking down on me is for psychological benefit as well as strategy.*

Dolan began to clap. Slow at first with pauses in between but growing steadily faster and louder until it was a full-on applause with a standing ovation. Normally, Dolan preferred to ambush his victims, but not tonight. Tonight was special. Tonight he would converse with his prey before creating his final and legendary masterpiece.

"Congratulations, James. Well played and well done. I see you brought a friend. How lovely. That's my fault. I said no pistol, but I failed to say no axe. I'll have to remember that next time. I like your choice of weaponry though, very much. So primitive and primal, an up close and personal weapon. Excellent choice, James, excellent." James had made no attempt to hide the axe. That was impossible even had he wanted to. But he didn't want to hide it anyway. He wanted the man to see what he had planned for him.

Where's Shelia?" he demanded.

"Why, she's right here." He motioned toward the bedroom. "I brought her home from the hospital for you. She's resting peacefully." The thought of this man touching his wife, being in his home, and the smirk on his face made his skin crawl. Now not only anger rose, but hate began to grow stronger with it in unison.

"You're a sick, twisted individual who enjoys torture and killing. I've witnessed it firsthand all night long. You love it. You say you're some kind of hero or avenging angel, but I say you're as twisted as they are. You use their sins as an excuse to indulge in your own. Who gave you the right to take it upon yourself to pass judgment?"

"I gave me the right! Me." For the first time tonight, Dolan's smirk was forced away. "I find human waste of life and I extinguish it. Snuff it out before they can do more evil, and in doing so, I have a little fun. Besides, the punishment I hand out is deserved. The greater the crime, the greater the course of action that need be taken. I take it you don't agree with my methods?" he asked as his smirk reappeared, and he began walking toward the head of the staircase as James was positioned only a few feet beyond the first step below.

"I agree that everyone I came across tonight deserved to die, yes, but not the way you did it. That was not punishment or vengeance. That was pure sadistic evil."

"And what those men did to all those innocent children wasn't evil? What if it had been your daughter who was sold and raped repeatedly until she cried out begging to die? I bet you would want to kill anyone who did that to your child, wouldn't you, James?" The fact that he was even mentioning his daughter made his temper flare even more.

"Yes, I'd want to kill them. But I wouldn't spend hours torturing them and mutilating their bodies."

Dolan began descending the staircase. "So it's okay to kill them, just not the way I done it. Is that what I'm hearing?"

"Yes. I mean no. I mean you can't call what you do justice." The anger and hate that was fueling him was starting to fog his thought process, making rational thought or intelligent conversation difficult. All he could think about was killing.

"So you agree with my process but not the method? That's a little wishy-washy, Charlie Brown." Dolan grinned as he took another step down.

"What do you want from me?" James demanded.

"What do I want? I want you to pay your price, James, the price for your involvement."

"For what! I don't even know these sick bastards. Neither does Shelia. What are you talking about?"

Dolan stopped almost a quarter of the way down the stairwell and gave pause for thought. "All these men lived on your properties, James. I know you have a property manager who makes your decisions for you on many things, and trust me, he will be dealt with as well. I have a special game just for him. But you are the owner and should care more about who is occupying your establishments rather than just collecting the rent. Maybe you didn't know about their past, and I'm positive you weren't aware of what was going on, but that's the point. You should have cared more, James. Cared about who and what you were enabling." Again, Dolan began his descent. "And that is why you must pay. Your death will not be as gruesome as those you've witnessed this evening, but it will be exceptional, as will Shelia's. And the display will be exquisite. Too bad you won't be able to enjoy it." Still descending slowly, Dolan was just over halfway down as he folded both hands behind his back.

James watched as he descended further. The axe he had held tight with the head facing down, he now let slide through his palm

THE WRITER

slowly, allowing gravity to do its job, until it reached his desired destination. Now he had a grip that was more to his liking.

Continuing down the staircase, Dolan spoke, "We all have to make decisions, James. Some people can live with their choices, and some people get butchered and killed for theirs." Again, more smirking. "What about you? Can you live with your choices? The axe, for instance, I'm sure you didn't bring it for nothing. You intend to kill me with it, obviously. If you succeed in doing so, what would that make you then? Would that not make you the same as me, a killer, as you say? Who gives you the right to kill me?"

"I'm nothing like you, nothing!" James shouted.

"But if you use that axe, you will be. Can you live with that choice? People like me—well, actually, I'm one of a kind, but for the sake of argument, people like me usually have no conscience. You, though, people like you, who do have a conscience, will you be able to live with yourself, James?" he asked with his smug grin.

Suddenly, all that mattered was wiping that smirk off his face. He hated it. He hated this game. He hated this conversation. Most of all, he hated this man, an all-consuming hate that was filling him, fueling him. All he wanted to do was erase that smirk from his face, as well erase this psycho from existence. The anger and hate were overwhelming him now. Engulfing him and feeding him to destroy. His grip on reality was fading as the grip on the axe tightened.

The Writer was only a few steps from the marble floor entry now. James continued to listen to his senseless babblings as he smirked. What he couldn't see was the hands behind his back unfolding and one free hand removing a syringe from his back pocket. "Is it hot in here or am I crazy?" Dolan asked, then laughed without letting his eyes leave James. "Perhaps you think you've been punished enough. Maybe you think you can hold me here until the police arrive, who are most certainly on their way. After all, they've been behind you every step of the way, getting closer as the night lingered. They are assuredly not far behind now."

Stepping off the stairs and onto marble, he was mere feet away from his prized trophy. James did not retreat backward, only stood firm with boiling hatred and sized up the killer. Both men were close to the same height and build, neither displaying a noticeable weakness.

"Maybe you don't think you should be punished at all, am I right? What if I allowed you to live and only punished Shelia instead? Leaving you to live the rest of your life knowing that it all took place under your roof, living in torment knowing that you failed to save your wife. And she died because of you. Maybe that should be your punishment instead of what I had initially planned." Dolan paused for thought. "Yes, I think so. I will allow you to live and wallow in your misery and failure to protect what was yours. For the rest of your life, you will live with regret knowing you couldn't save her. Congratulations, you win. Now though, I'm afraid we must part ways so I can make proper preparations, since you've altered my plans. I do have to thank you though for such a splendid idea. I wish I had thought of it on my own. I guess sometimes a person can get tunnel vision. Thank you."

Now standing less than three feet apart, Dolan moved with uncanny speed to deliver the syringe to James's neck. With a speed even faster than his, James raised the axe over his head and delivered a blow directly between Dolan's eyes, cutting through his skull. As he was rearing back, his left arm came up the same time Dolan was trying to administer his homemade cocktail with his right and inadvertently blocked the needle from reaching its intended target and instead stuck in his arm before breaking off. The syringe fell to the ground with only a small portion of the needle penetrating through his coat into the skin and with very little concoction actually entering the bloodstream.

The sound the axe made was so satisfactory James smiled and wanted to hear it again. Though the blow landed dead-on, the smirk remained on his face. All the anger now spilled out of James as he pulled the axe free and began to create a masterpiece of his own. This time, James drew back with both hands, made a full swing, and delivered another blow. Again, the axe rang true, landing where the previous blow had struck, driving in deeper, and further separating the wound.

THE WRITER

This time, the blow drove through to the bottom jaw, sending teeth flying like shrapnel along with splintered bone and red confetti. Even with the face now cut almost in two, the lips on either side of the blade were curled into what looked to James to be a smirk. Falling to his knees, Dolan looked up at James. Pulling the axe out, James delivered a third blow, this time further back on the cranium. The skull split wider, sending small chunks of membrane jetting through the air, and the blood flowed.

Pulling the axe away, the body fell to the floor, twitching and convulsing. James hadn't realized he'd begun to laugh, almost hysterically. Blood was shooting out, painting the walls, railings, and spraying James, yet the laughter grew. Again, he withdrew the axe and brought it down, finding solace in its destruction. The head was basically in two pieces now, Dolan certainly dead, but James had lost connection with all reality. He had become someone else now.

The axe withdrew and landed again, withdrew and landed again. Withdraw, swing, destroy, withdraw, swing destroy. No longer in control, helpless to stop, he kept chopping. Relentlessly, he continued cutting away at the evil on the ground. He was hitting on all cylinders now, going to town. Swing, destroy, swing, destroy, laughing the entire time. James had even begun to talk to Dolan as he tried to erase him, having no knowledge of doing so. Swing, destroy, swing, destroy. *Erase him, vanquish him, remove him*, he thought, laughing like a madman as he chopped.

The entryway was soaked in blood. James was drenched in it. Still, he chopped. The adrenaline wouldn't allow him to stop nor the madness. Ribs snapped, bones severed, organs turned to pulp with the continuing blows that rained down. The axe was playing sweet music to his ears, and he wanted to hear more.

Swing, erase, swing, erase, swing, erase. Head, arms, hands, torso all chopped into kibble. What lay in the floor was equivalent to raw burger. Still, he chopped, mostly just moving pieces around now. So little was left, at least from the waist up. Maximum carnage.

James delivered blows until he could no longer raise his arms. Exhausted, he fell back against the wall and balanced himself before he could fall into the mess he had created. Not that it would have made much difference. He was covered in the fluid from head to toe. Sometime during the process of erasing Dolan, James's laughter had turned to crying. Now he was spent and trying to catch his breath not only from the countless number of blows he delivered but as well the hysteria that had enveloped him.

Using his coat, he wiped away at blood on his face (which did little good since it too was covered) as he stared at what was laying before him. His mind still not coherent, he stood gazing into the red pool of death knowing nothing, only staring. *I should have saved enough energy to do the rest.* He finally had thought. *Must erase.* James tried lifting the axe, but his arms felt as though they were a thousand pounds each. His mind was in a fog, a haze of uncomprehending.

In the distance, James heard sirens. Far away still and faint, but the sound helped bring him slowly back somewhat from where his mind had been. Now that the music from his axe had ceased, the siren's drones were able to be realized. Like coming out of a dream, or in this case a nightmare, James's thoughts began to change from revenge, killing, slicing, and erasing to an emotion completely opposite of all those.

In his weakened state, the anger and hate dispensed as his thoughts went to Shelia. "Shelia," he said aloud but feebly. Trying to erect himself from his slouched position against the wall, he tried to muster more volume in his voice. "Shelia." Still a weak call, but better than the previous. His mind gathering more focus and fresh adrenaline beginning to flow, he stood straight up now and bellowed. "Shelia." No reply came. "Please, God, don't let her be dead, please."

Looking up at the top of the staircase thinking it was a hundred miles away, he began the climb, stepping to the first stair. His shoes soaked with blood made him lose traction. Using both hands to catch his fall, the right one still clutching the axe, he caught hold of the fifth step, preventing him from busting his face. Fortunately, the axe blade was turned horizontally as he landed, running lengthways with the stairs, or he would have received a troubling cut himself.

Regaining his footing, he tried again, this time more careful as his mind was starting the reboot process of rational thought. One step at a time, he went, sliding some with the shoes so wet and the blood covering the stairs already but not losing traction again. He looked like someone trying to ice-skate for the first time, feet sliding either way, clutching the railing all the way to the top of the stairwell, calling her name as he ascended.

Once he reached the summit, the sirens again captured his attention. Closer now but still a fair distance away. *Are they coming here?* he wondered. *Of course they're coming here, you moron. There's no one else out here for miles around. That's one of the reasons we chose it.* Turning to his left, he walked toward the master bedroom, dragging the axe, which left a trail of blood on the floor along with his footsteps.

Something was sticking him in the left arm. Pausing to take a look, he reached under his jacket and felt the obstruction. Grabbing hold, he pulled it free and held it up to the light. "What is this?" he asked himself aloud. "Looks like the end of a needle." James hadn't noticed what Dolan had pulled from behind his back when they were standing face to face. From the point he raised the axe, he had focused only on one thing—killing.

Fantastic. What was in that? he wondered. *How much was distributed before the needle broke? Is this how he captured his prey, by injecting them first? It doesn't matter,* he told himself. *I have to see If Shelia's alive.* Continuing toward the room, he dropped the broken needle and lifted the axe. Somewhat getting a second wind, he was anxious to find out her condition. However, he wondered what he'd been dosed with and how much. Maybe he would still die, but not before he saw her.

Approaching the bedroom, he noticed a small piece of paper folded over and stuck to the door, a piece of stationery from their nightstand. Opening the paper, already knowing it was from the Writer, James read three words. "You chose poorly."

The door left ajar exposed a small crack to peer through. James dropped the note and pushed the door open slowly, afraid of what he would find. Inch by inch, it crept until full view of the room was showing. The sirens blared, getting close now and coming quickly. He still had time.

James stepped into the room and saw Shelia lying on the bed, arms folded over her chest, looking as if she were a cadaver in a casket. "No, no, no," he cried. *This can't be happening again. What has he done to you? Maybe she was only drugged.* Shot with the same drug that was flowing in his very veins now. Yes, that was it. Had to be. She couldn't be dead. Not after everything he had been through—all the anguish, misery, and horror. Not after all he'd endured. She couldn't be dead. It wasn't possible. The madman could not win. Surely not after everything that had happened. "You don't get to win!" he screamed into the open air.

The sirens screamed, piercing the air. Afraid to approach her and confirm that the psycho had won and killed her, James only stood watching her. Then slowly, her chest rose, inhaling life-giving air. The tears of sorrow he had been shedding now turned to tears of hope. A smile touched his lips. As she exhaled, his smile became a small laugh of promise. Still, he hadn't moved. "Thank you, God," he spoke aloud.

Maybe everything was going to turn out all right after all. Sure, he would have a lot of explaining to do, but they were both still alive. *Whatever he stuck in my veins couldn't be fatal. The needle had broken off before it could be lethal,* he told himself. *I'll hire the best attorneys money can buy. After they see everything this sicko has done, no court would convict me. Impossible.*

Still holding the axe, he started his approach toward the bed. As he took the first step, a small numb sensation started in his feet, slowly working its way up the backs of his legs, past his beltline, crawling up his back, growing hotter as it rose, up over his shoulders, past his neck, before flooding his brain. His vision went to a complete whiteout. The whitest white he'd ever seen. His mind filled with nothingness.

James came to standing inside his master bedroom gripping a bloody double-headed axe as it dripped fresh blood into a puddle on the custom tile. He had no recollection of how he came to be here or where he came from. His mind was blank. Frozen in terror, slowly, he turned only his head to follow the trail of blood which led out of the room and trailed back behind him before disappearing at the top of the stairwell. What or who was at the bottom of the staircase? He asked himself. Surely, whatever it was had to be dead, butchered more likely, by the looks of the thick trail of red liquid splatters neighboring the bloody footprints that led to his own feet.

James turned toward the woods approximately three hundred yards away and did the only thing he could do…RUN!

About the Author

Phil lives in Cincinnati, Ohio, with his wife and daughter, where he owns and operates his own home-restoration company, which is where many of the influences and ideas came from to bring this short novel to fruition. Although the book is fiction, many truths are peppered throughout its pages.

Printed in the USA
CPSIA information can be obtained
at www.ICGtesting.com
LVHW091742041123
762971LV00045B/512